The r... ...rld—
a fam... ...ood and passion,
tor... ...t by deceit and desire.

Niroli—present-day vision of the island

With all it has to offer, who wouldn't be tempted by a holiday on the island of Niroli? There are beautiful sandy beaches, especially around the new development area on the south coast, where you will find top-of-the-range luxury hotels, casinos, restaurants and bars for a relaxing holiday. The island has a rich history—don't miss the chance to explore its wonderful Roman ruins. In the northeast part of the island, there is a Roman amphitheater, where concerts are still performed today, particularly during the traditional annual festivals. Visitors must see the stunning main town of Niroli. If you enter the port by boat, it is particularly impressive, as you see the town sprawling up the hillside in front of you, with the historic palace just in view. Do wander round the old town and soak up the atmosphere.

The Official Fierezza Family Tree

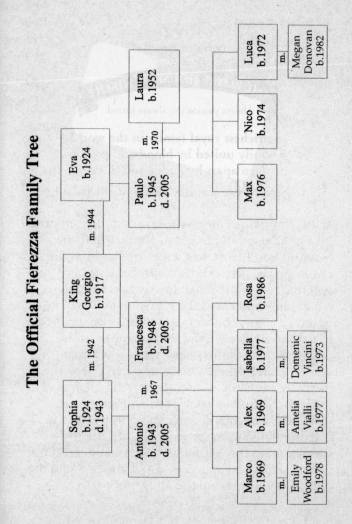

SUSAN STEPHENS

Expecting His Royal Baby

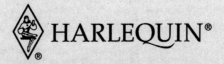

HARLEQUIN®

TORONTO • NEW YORK • LONDON
AMSTERDAM • PARIS • SYDNEY • HAMBURG
STOCKHOLM • ATHENS • TOKYO • MILAN • MADRID
PRAGUE • WARSAW • BUDAPEST • AUCKLAND

For everyone involved in this exciting journey
to Niroli, especially Jenny and The Team at
Harlequin Mills & Boon

ISBN-13: 978-0-373-38955-1
ISBN-10: 0-373-38955-8

EXPECTING HIS ROYAL BABY

First North American Publication 2007.

Copyright © 2007 by Harlequin Books S.A.

Special thanks and acknowledgment are given to Susan Stephens for her contribution to THE ROYAL HOUSE OF NIROLI series.

www.eHarlequin.com

Printed in U.S.A.

The Rules

Rule 1: The ruler must be a moral leader. Any act that brings the Royal House into disrepute will rule a contender out of the succession to the throne.

Rule 2: No member of the Royal House may be joined in marriage without consent of the ruler. Any such union concluded results in exclusion and deprivation of honors and privileges.

Rule 3: No marriage is permitted if the interests of Niroli become compromised through the union.

Rule 4: It is not permitted for the ruler of Niroli to marry a person who has previously been divorced.

Rule 5: Marriage between members of the Royal House who are blood relations is forbidden.

Rule 6: The ruler directs the education of all members of the Royal House, even when the general care of the children belongs to their parents.

Rule 7: Without the approval or consent of the ruler, no member of the Royal House can make debts over the possibility of payment.

Rule 8: No member of the Royal House can accept an inheritance or any donation without the consent and approval of the ruler.

Rule 9: The ruler of Niroli must dedicate their life to the Kingdom. Therefore they are not permitted to have a profession.

Rule 10: Members of the Royal House must reside in Niroli or in a country approved by the ruler. However, the ruler *must* reside in Niroli.

THE ROYAL HOUSE OF NIROLI

Always passionate, always proud.

Harlequin Presents is delighted to bring you an exciting installment from THE ROYAL HOUSE OF NIROLI, in which you can follow the epic search for the true Nirolian king. Eight heirs, eight romances, eight fantastic stories!

Maximillian—the last known heir to the throne.
Will a beautiful girl, bound to him by a scandalous family secret, prevent him from becoming king?

PROLOGUE

As HE WATCHED the tiny dot appear through the clouds the ambassador of Niroli's throat dried. What if this precious heir to the throne should perish? And with Nico Fierezza's addiction to extreme sports that seemed extremely likely; if not today, then some day soon. The ambassador's nerves refused to steady even when the dot turned into six feet four of solid muscle and Nico hit the ground on target. Only Nico didn't *hit* the ground, he landed like a cat.

As someone took away his parachute Nico lifted off his helmet and stared straight at the ambassador. He had detected the distinguished visitor in the same instant he had located the cross hairs on his jumping target and was relieved to see that duty rather than disaster had brought him to the field.

He maintained a distance between himself and the bickering and power play surrounding his grandfather, King Giorgio of Niroli. The Fierezza family had ruled Niroli since the Middle Ages, but Nico was a self-made man. Niroli, a tiny island set like a jewel in the Mediterranean, was prosperous and beautiful enough to attract the glitterati from every part of the world, which was enough in itself to keep him away. He had built up his own architectural practice in London free from royal privilege or favour and could state categorically that everything he owned he had earned.

He had been drunk on adrenalin when he'd landed, feeling invincible because he'd survived against the odds the highest jump without oxygen ever recorded, but calm reason had kicked in reminding him that, like any emotion, euphoria was a dangerous deception; it clouded the mind.

Tucking his helmet under his arm, he started forward with his usual purposeful stride. He couldn't account for the insatiable force driving him. He'd had a happy childhood, idyllic compared to most, with a mother who adored him and poured all her love into the family. Perhaps that was it, Nico thought, halting at a point where he and the ambassador could have some privacy, perhaps men like him came with an inborn gene that insisted they must break away from everything that was feminine and soft and loving and drive themselves to the limit just to know they were alive. His father had done this, taking his yacht to the limit of its capabilities, killing himself along with his brother and sister-in-law. It was a miracle his mother had survived and was a lesson he would never forget.

As the ambassador approached Nico ordered himself to go easy on the man, but there could be no compromise. He might be the grandson of the king, but he neither asked for nor expected any favours. 'Ambassador?' he said curtly as the portly man arrived.

'You recognised me…' The ambassador gave a nervous laugh.

'Of course.' Nico's voice was clipped and controlled. As always he was polite, toning down his need to know in deference to the other man's advanced age. 'My mother?'

'Is quite well, sir. Your grandfather too….'

Nico's brow furrowed. Why the hesitation? As if he didn't

know. 'His Majesty wishes to see me.' It was a statement rather than a question. Nico never wasted his breath on unnecessary questions.

'That is correct, sir.'

The ambassador was distracted briefly by the whoops of celebration from other skydivers in the competition. Nico's had been a landslide victory, but he remained unmoved, his thoughts hidden behind his slate-blue gaze.

As he stroked one hand across the sun-bleached hair he kept aggressively short, Nico had no idea how intimidating he appeared to the older man. Lean and tanned from working outside in all weather, Nico Fierezza towered a good six inches over the ambassador. It didn't matter that an architectural scheme had been conceived in the clinical surroundings of his high-tech office—Nico liked to see his cutting-edge designs up close. So while the ambassador's hands were soft and white, Nico's were weather-beaten and rough, and the ambassador hardly seemed to have a beard in contrast to Nico's black, piratical stubble. But the ambassador worked for a wily monarch and was used to handling every type of situation. He had recovered from his trot across the airfield and his shrewd grey eyes missed nothing. He rested super alert like a pulsing brain as Nico began to speak.

'Please tell His Majesty that I will attend him the moment my business allows.'

As a cheer went up and calls rang out for Nico to join the other men on the podium he made a holding gesture with the flat of his hand.

The ambassador weighed the facts. Nico Fierezza was easily the best of all the men there. Surely, he must be feeling the same charge they did, the same adrenalin rush? And yet he appeared to be in no hurry to join the celebrations and there was no hint of self-congratulation in his expression. He'd heard this grandson to the king was a stranger to emotion, and it seemed the rumours were true. Nothing could have suited his purpose better. King Giorgio was eager to put an heir in place before his health deteriorated further, and this man had all the qualities they looked for in a monarch. He put duty first and chose to reveal nothing to the outside world. There wasn't a woman alive who could cause Nico Fierezza embarrassment. The ambassador maintained his impassive expression, but inwardly he was already celebrating.

'Please apologise to His Majesty,' Nico continued, 'and tell him that I will attend him in Niroli at the earliest opportunity.'

The ambassador dipped his head. Compromise was an easy thing with victory in sight. 'His Majesty will understand. He has empowered me to ask you to attend him at a time convenient to yourself.'

The hint of a smile fed into Nico's stern gaze. Since when had King Giorgio been any more accommodating than he was? His grandfather had to be desperate to see him if he was prepared to wait. 'It may be one week, or two,' he said, 'but no longer than that.'

'That's excellent news,' the ambassador said. 'I'm sure His Majesty will be delighted.' A flicker in Nico's eyes warned him not to overstate the case. 'Perhaps if we could settle on a date,' he added.

'I'll let you know.' Nico's voice had turned hard. His message was clear: one concession was enough for today. 'If you'll excuse me, Ambassador…'

As he strode away Nico didn't see the ambassador dip into the type of bow he normally reserved for the king.

CHAPTER ONE

THERE WAS A single white rose on a coffin splattered with raindrops....

It made Carrie sad to see the tender bloom lying on the brass plate that spoke to a world that would never read it: the name of an aunt who had never loved her. But love could not be controlled at will, and Carrie had loved her aunt in spite of the woman's rejection of her. Sad as she was, Carrie was glad there were some things words could never destroy and that love was one of them.

'Carrie Evans?'

Carrie turned to find a man standing behind her. He was sheltering beneath the oily spread of a black umbrella, which made the shadows on his saturnine face all the deeper, adding to his air of gloom. There were only four people at her aunt's funeral other than herself—the minister and three undertakers—and it was hard to feel brave as the small group peeled away to allow her some privacy. Lifting up her chin, she gazed squarely into the face of the man. 'I'm Carrie Evans. Can I help you?'

'Sorry, miss... I tried the house.'

Carrie didn't know the man, but she could guess what he had come for. He was here to serve papers evicting her from her aunt's house on the instructions of relatives who hadn't been to visit Aunt Mabel in Carrie's living memory. A solicitor had rung her yesterday to explain.

Yesterday, the day when everything in her life had changed for good….

Carrie was twenty-five, but she looked much younger. Her complexion was pale and she dressed conservatively, keeping her luxuriant hair scraped back neatly in a practical twist. She found the lush tresses an embarrassment. Her natural hair colour was a rich golden red that painters called titian, and she believed it better suited to an actress or a glamour model. She had even thought about dying her hair a pale shade of brown, but the upkeep would have been too much on a secretary's salary. Her eyes were large and cornflower-blue and were perhaps her most expressive feature. Widely set and fringed with sable lashes, they were quick to darken with emotion, but could turn steely when there was something or someone to defend.

The man addressing Carrie saw a capable young woman, a little too plump to ever be called stylish, but determined, nonetheless, he concluded.

'I have already cleared my belongings from my late aunt's house,' she told him without rancour, 'and as soon as we're finished here I will collect my suitcase and deliver the house keys to my aunt's solicitor….'

She couldn't do any more, and he felt some sympathy for her. He'd heard she had nowhere to go since her aunt's heirs had turned up and laid claim to the house where she lived. 'You're so well organised,' he said, trying to soften the blow for her, 'I hardly need to give you this….'

'I think you do,' she told him.

Her tone was serious and exposed his attempt to console

her for the sham it was. She held his gaze as she reached for the documents he was carrying and, as he handed over the eviction notice, he couldn't help thinking that, in spite of the downturn in her fortunes, the young woman in front of him possessed a quiet dignity that commanded his respect.

She had forgotten how cold and bare her attic room was. The eviction notice allowed her twenty-four hours to clear out her things. She neither wanted nor needed twenty-four hours. She missed her aunt, but she was pleased to be leaving such a sad and lonely place. Her aunt's house could so easily have been filled with love and laughter if only Aunt Mabel had been able to forget that Carrie's father had chosen Carrie's mother over herself.

But things could be worse. Carrie's mouth tipped down wryly as she totted up the facts. She was jobless, homeless, single and pregnant.

Carrie's wry smile turned into a smile of true happiness when she thought about her baby. The pregnancy was a source of great joy to her that nothing could dim. She was going to have someone to love; someone who would love her, someone she could care for and champion. The only problem was her baby's father. He would have to be told. He had a right to know, Carrie thought, even as her stomach clenched with apprehension.

Unfortunately, her baby's father was the hardest and most unfeeling man she had ever known. He was about as approachable as a tiger with a thorn in its pad. He was also the man she was in love with, the man she had loved since the first moment she had set eyes on him; the only man she could ever love... The same man who barely knew she was alive. And the longer she left it, the harder it would be to tell him that he was about to become a father.

Crossing her arms over her stomach in a protective gesture, Carrie determined she would not allow anything to stand in the way of her baby's future happiness, certainly not her own lack of nerve. She had to face up to him and she would. She didn't want anything for herself, but she did want recognition and security for her child. Her baby's father was a very wealthy man and she wondered if he could be persuaded to set up a trust fund to provide for college fees when the time came.

Before Carrie had learned she was pregnant she had dreamed of leaving the office where she had worked as a secretary to try and turn her hobby of painting into a profession, but that was out of the question now. She planned instead to find some cheap accommodation and work until the baby came. Her goal was to build up a small nest egg so that one day she could buy a modest property with a child-friendly garden. A solid base was important. She didn't want a child of hers to be pushed from pillar to post as she had been after her parents' tragic accident. She might be homeless today, but not for long.

Nico Fierezza. It was the only name the King of Niroli had allowed to be spoken in his presence for days, and he had just been informed that his grandson Nico was on the final flight path to Niroli.

Nico piloting his own jet… King Giorgio's mouth curved with appreciation. Nico lived the life he would have enjoyed had not royal duty claimed him. And now the only task remaining in his long and eventful life was to tame this wild grandson of his and persuade him to accept the throne.

Tame Nico Fierezza? King Giorgio's eyes clouded over. Even a king might find that a challenge. Then his crafty gaze brightened. Maybe there wasn't a man alive who could tame Nico Fierezza, but a woman might…

* * *

What was he doing in Niroli? Nico asked himself as he brought his jet down in a perfect landing. What was he doing back on this small, lush, glamorous island? Niroli, the island of dreams for so many, but not for him.

He was happy to undertake the odd restoration project of the sort he had recently completed for his cousin Isabella, or even to design major projects like the new airport-terminal building. But his life was in London. The only things he had missed about Niroli were his mother, Princess Laura, and his brothers, Luca and Max. His younger brother, Max, was fully committed to the wine groves he cared for, and his older brother, Luca, owned the casino that contributed so much to the island's wealth. Luca had run the casino himself for years, but after a whirlwind romance he had recently married and moved to his bride's native Australia to develop his business interests over there. Nico was the only member of his family to have inherited the restless gene, and right now that gene was killing him, urging him to leave the island before he had even halted the jet.

Nico's lips tightened with impatience as he taxied in to the premier spot. They had laid out the red carpet for him. When would they ever learn that pomp and ceremony were the very last things that would lure him back to Niroli? But this was his first visit to the island since the tragedy of the yachting accident. Half his immediate family gone and the weight of their loss still hung heavily on him. Was his time so precious he couldn't spare any for his remaining family?

He would do what he could to reassure his ageing grandfather and then he'd spend some time with the rest of his family. But not too much time. He didn't want to raise false hope. He could do the maths as well as anyone. There were three surviving male heirs ahead of him, and he had no doubt they had all found some reason to exclude themselves from the succession, which meant he was next on the list.

Why else would his grandfather want to see him?

Whatever King Giorgio's reason, it didn't change a thing; he wasn't interested in the throne.

Nico's reasons for refusing the throne of Niroli went far beyond his restless nature. He wouldn't accept anything under false pretences and knew that the last thing Niroli needed was another king desperately casting about for an heir some time in the future. A childhood illness had left him infertile, which meant marriage and long-term relationships had always been out of the question. He didn't dwell on it, and in some ways it suited him, because he didn't answer to anyone.

She couldn't tell the father of her baby the news over the telephone. She had no alternative other than to face the lion in his den....

Lifting her suitcase as the underground train slowed to a halt, Carrie squeezed her way through the press of commuters. When she finally saw the light of day again she put her suitcase down and turned her collar up. It was a typical summer's day in London with rain sheeting down from pewter skies. And every cab was taken, which was hardly a surprise. One drop of rain was always enough to ensure that was the case, and this was a full-blown summer storm.

Picking up her bag, Carrie started to walk at a brisk pace towards the commercial centre of the city where she had been employed as a secretary. It seemed so long ago, though it had only been three months since she had left her job on a point of principle.

More pride than principle, Carrie accepted, shivering with cold. Aunt Mabel, never one to miss an opportunity, had immediately dismissed her nursing staff and hired Carrie in their place. It was a job Carrie had been pleased to do. Aunt Mabel hadn't paid her, but at least she had felt useful, as if she was earning the right to her board and lodgings, though, of course, she had paid for those, too. In her naïvety, she had hoped by working for her aunt it would bring them closer.

She knew better than to expect miracles now, but whatever happened she would cope with it. Apart from sharing the news of her pregnancy with her baby's father, she was after a reference. With a baby to support she had to find something more than casual work and had left her job in such a hurry she had overlooked the practicalities. Where had her brain been?

Somewhere below Nico Fierezza's belt, Carrie accepted grimly as she shouldered her way into his sleek steel-and-glass office building. She had been so overwhelmed by Nico noticing her at all that she had been swept into a fantasy of her own making without any thought of the consequences.

The first discovery Carrie made was that the girl who had once been her assistant was now office supervisor. Meek and mild to haughty in twelve weeks flat, which wasn't bad going, Carrie conceded as she braved the girl's disdainful stare.

'Not there.' The emery board that had been busily sawing at some impressive red talons took a break. 'If you leave your case there it will drip on the carpet.'

'I seem to be doing that, anyway,' Carrie pointed out, holding onto her composure by the thinnest of threads. 'Do you mind if I take off my coat and hang it up to dry?'

The girl shrugged.

'Is Nico in?'

'Mr Fierezza? I'm afraid you can't just drop in here on the off chance that Mr Fierezza will see you. He's a very busy man. You will have to make a proper appointment.'

'I appreciate the fact that he's busy…' When was Nico not

busy? 'I'm prepared to wait if I have to, but would you mind telling him that I'm here?'

'Why can't I help you?' The girl's gaze sharpened as she looked at Carrie.

'Are you going to call him? Or shall I go straight in?' Straightening her back, Carrie left the girl in no doubt that she would.

'It won't help you to go—'

The girl moved faster than Carrie could have imagined, leaping in front of her to bar the way to Nico's office. 'He isn't here,' she said smugly.

Carrie's shoulders slumped. The news was a real blow.

'Carrie!'

Carrie's heart lifted as she turned to see an older woman advancing on them like a galleon in full sail.

'Great to see you, Carrie! What are you doing here?' Linking arms, she led Carrie away.

Carrie couldn't believe her luck. Sonia Farraday was one of her favourite people. Legend had it that Sonia came with the building, but Carrie knew that Sonia was the hub around which everything in Nico's London office revolved when he was away.

'Let me get you a hot drink—you're soaked through,' Sonia insisted. 'Come into my den. And, Shelley…' Sonia's voice hardened '…find a cloth and dry off Carrie's suitcase.

'Honestly,' Sonia added as she bustled Carrie into her pin-neat room, 'young women these days!' Her gutsy laugh proved exactly why Carrie liked her so much. 'Now then, what can I do for you?' Sonia demanded once they were both seated.

'I need to speak to Nico, Sonia.'

'Hmm.' Sonia sat back. 'That's not so easy. Nico isn't in London and he won't be back for some time. As soon as he's tied up all the loose ends on his latest project Nico's going to visit his family in Niroli. There are rumours he may stay there indefinitely,' she confided with a meaningful glance.

'In Niroli?' Carrie paled.

'He doesn't share everything with me. Nico keeps his private life private, as you know. He'll tell me what he intends to do when he's ready and not before.' Sonia's shrewd gaze sharpened as it rested on Carrie's face. 'Why don't you let me get you that drink now? You look worn out. When I come back we'll have another chat, and then I'll make some calls and see if I can help you….'

Carrie nodded dumbly as Sonia left her. Nico living in Niroli was a complication she hadn't factored into her thinking. And now she had aroused Sonia's curiosity, and she didn't want to confide in her. It wasn't that she didn't trust Sonia, but Nico had to be the first to know about their baby.

As she sat waiting in the office Carrie stared thoughtfully at the computer. Nico's address in Niroli would be there somewhere, and if her password hadn't changed she could bring it up on the screen….

It only took her a few minutes and then she sat back stunned by what she had discovered. Nico didn't have an address in Niroli; not as such—he kept an apartment at the palace. She had known Nico was the king's grandson, but perhaps because he had never made anything of it she had always thought of him as a lesser royal, a man whose connections to the glittering court were so distant as to be insignificant. But now she knew better. Nico Fierezza was not only a member of the ruling family of Niroli, he lived in the palace.

Her baby's father lived in a palace!

It made her mission to find Nico a lot bigger challenge, but not impossible, Carrie determined as Sonia bustled back into the room with a tray of coffee. 'Now, drink this up,' Sonia told her warmly. 'You look as if you've seen a ghost. Are you sure you're looking after yourself properly, Carrie?'

Sonia was fishing, Carrie realised. 'I'm doing fine. It's just so cold outside.'

'You should be back in this nice warm office. We miss you.'

It was another prompt, Carrie realised, but she couldn't accept the opening Sonia was giving her. She could never work for Nico again after what had happened between them.

When they had finished their coffee Sonia was as good as her word, and it only took a couple of calls for her to establish that Nico was in Niroli.

Niroli. The island was a legend. It was a smarter and more glamorous world than she could ever imagine. Nico belonging there made him seem more remote and unapproachable than ever.

Sensing Carrie's reluctance to talk, Sonia didn't press her, but when the time came for her to leave, Sonia insisted, 'You mustn't walk to the underground in this weather, Carrie, or you'll catch your death of cold. I'm going to call a cab for you. Are you still at the same address?'

As Sonia's hand hovered over the telephone receiver Carrie accepted that what the older woman had told her changed everything, but she couldn't embroil Sonia in her difficulties. She had a child to protect now and must stand on her own two feet. 'If you could call a taxi that would be great, but if you don't mind I'll decide where I'm going when it gets here….'

CHAPTER TWO

IT WASN'T as if she had any ties holding her in England, Carrie reflected as the plane banked steeply on the final approach to Niroli and, in spite of her apprehension, she couldn't suppress her excitement at the thought of seeing Nico again. Her hands tightened around the in-flight magazine in which she had found pictures of the palace taken from the air. Just the thought of trying to gain entrance to somewhere so splendid made her heart race. The question was, could she do it?

She had to do it, Carrie determined, stuffing the magazine back in its net. Staring out of the window, she tried to distract herself. She could see the bright blue ocean far below dotted with tiny boats and, in the distance, the coastline of Niroli, edged with pale golden sand. The island looked so tranquil from the sky she didn't want to think about the drama that was about to unfold, but she wouldn't dodge it, either. There was some irony in the situation. When Nico had hired her he'd said it was her quiet perseverance that had brought her to his notice, and now that same determination was about to be turned against him….

She was pregnant because they'd had sex at the office party. It was such a cliché, she could hardly believe it herself, but she had always been ready for Nico; he'd only had to look at her a certain way. She had been hovering on the fringes of the party with a wineglass in her hand. She wasn't good at small talk, the words would never come quickly enough, and if they did, they were invariably the wrong words. People couldn't be bothered to wait while she tried to find something witty or fascinating to say. She hadn't drunk a lot, just a glass or two of wine. In fact, she had been wondering how soon she could slip away without causing offence. It had been during one of those 'poised for flight' moments that Nico had sought her out.

'All alone, Carrie?'

Her heart performed a perfect somersault. Nico Fierezza had never spoken to her outside office hours. Yet he'd been there standing right next to her, so close she could smell his cologne and could separate each complex note: musk, sandalwood, vanilla and an additional edge of something that hinted of warm water and toothpaste and long, hot, soapy showers—

'Daydreaming?' He'd broken into her thoughts with that low, husky voice that'd always made her tremble inwardly when she was taking notes for him.

'That's not like you, Carrie,' he'd observed.

The note of censure had made her stare up into slate-blue eyes she had never felt brave enough to study before. Then she'd seen they had a striking pewter ring around the iris and that the whites were very white against his tan.

'I've been watching you....'

The fact that he'd even noticed her was news, indeed, and the touch of humour in his voice had ensured that her attention remained fixed to his face. But, as usual, nothing sparkling had flown to her lips. It'd been the most exciting moment of her life and she'd been speechless. She'd taken in Nico's lashes, so long and thick and black like the stubble on his cheeks, and then her pulse had gone wild when he'd smiled into her eyes.

'Are you all right? Can I get you something before we land?'

Shocked into the present, Carrie gasped out loud. She had been gripping the seat arms, she realised, which the flight attendant had mistaken for nerves. 'Nothing, nothing, thank you….'

As the woman walked away Carrie tried to shut the memories out, but Nico's voice was in her head… Nico teasing her, Nico telling her she was his strait-laced secretary with the big innocent eyes and there were questions he wanted answered… She was spellbound that he was interested in anything other than her secretarial skills. And then he'd said something extraordinary: 'You must know you've been under my wing since you got here….'

Under Nico's wing? Her mind went into free fall. She'd hoarded up each time he'd smiled at her like a miser hoarding gold, but she'd always believed he was encouraging her to do better, to work harder….

'I love your modesty,' he'd gone on. 'I find subtlety in a woman incredibly attractive….'

Attractive? Nico found her attractive? His words had echoed in her head like a siren call. And then she'd found her voice, but only to stutter clumsily, 'I've not… I mean, I'm not…'

'If I've got this wrong just say the word…' His voice had been teasing.

What word? None came to mind.

'I want you, Carrie….'

The moment he'd said that she was lost. She wanted Nico so badly it hurt. And then he'd leaned back against the wall, his timing impeccable. She had been so sure he was about to take her in his arms that she swayed towards him, which was all the answer Nico had been looking for.

She might have made a sound when he'd removed the wineglass from her hand, but she was certainly struck dumb when he'd taken her from the party, lead her by the hand across the room. She'd followed him willingly; she would have followed him anywhere.

When they'd reached the boardroom he'd shut and locked the door. Then, gathering her to him, he'd used the lightest and most persuasive touch on her arms as if asking her permission to go further. She'd given it gladly. He hadn't needed to ask, her body'd melted like candle wax. She'd not only been willing, she'd been eager to serve. Nico Fierezza was a god amongst men. He was the only man she had ever wanted and it'd been a dream come true. He could have done anything with her.

Nico was everything she had imagined and more. He was tender, loving, considerate and hotter than a man had any right to be. While he'd dropped kisses on her neck above the chaste white barrier of her Peter Pan collar he'd freed the buttons on her blouse with long, deft fingers. Soothing and exciting her at the same time with his lips, tongue and teeth, he'd suggested all sorts of wickedness in husky Nirolian. She'd been so aroused she'd yelped in complaint when he'd paused to push her neatly tailored jacket from her shoulders. But as it was only a short pause, she'd forgiven him, and then her blouse was open to the waist and her heavy breasts in the fine lace bra were fully exposed for his perusal. She'd felt a moment's shame knowing her bras were far too small for her and she had been meaning to buy more, but the expression on Nico's face had told her to relax. He'd approved. He'd loved her breasts. He'd loved the way they'd spilled over the confining cups and he'd loved the fact that her nipples had been so engorged they'd pressed like tight red buds against the flimsy lace.

Arching her back, she'd thrust them towards him, making her breasts a gift to him, her first gift to Nico….

Carrie flinched now as the flight attendant lightly touched her hand.

'We've been forced to circle the airport, but we'll be down on the ground very soon….'

'Thank you for telling me.'

'A drink of water, perhaps?'

'I'm fine, honestly…just a little tense.' And just a little concerned that her guilty thoughts were an open book to the woman!

'It's understandable,' the flight attendant said sympathetically. 'There's been a lot of turbulence, but it's nothing to worry about. In ten minutes or so it will be all over and your holiday will have begun.'

Her holiday? If only! Carrie smiled. 'Thank you… I'm not usually so much trouble….'

'No trouble at all,' the flight attendant assured her, moving on to attend to another nervous passenger.

She couldn't allow herself to become distracted like this, Carrie told herself firmly. She had to make a conscious effort to blank Nico out of her mind. Closing her eyes, she concentrated on happy thoughts about the tiny child growing inside her until a light touch on her shoulder told her that the flight attendant was back with her water. 'You're very kind.'

'That's what we're here for.'

The small kindness brought tears to Carrie's eyes. She knew her hormones were to blame, but took it as a warning that she must be careful to keep a check on her feelings when she met Nico. She must give him no reason to think her weak.

She drank the water down quickly and closed her eyes, trying to shut her mind to everything, but soon she was drifting into the half world somewhere between waking and sleeping where Nico was waiting for her. She couldn't blame him for what had happened. She had been as eager as he that night and had turned from meltingly acquiescent to fiercely demanding in the space of a kiss….

Everyone knew Nico was strong, but that night she had discovered that his body felt like warm marble beneath her hands. The intimacy of touching his naked skin had given her an incredible charge. From that moment on she had been able to think of nothing but him sinking deep inside her.

Nico had known exactly what she'd wanted. His hands had been sure as they'd reached for the fastening on her skirt. She had encouraged him, laughing softly, nipping his skin with her small white teeth until he'd appeared to change his mind… Nico had had other plans for her. Swinging her into his arms, he had settled her on the edge of the boardroom table where she was at the perfect height for him. As he had nudged his way between her thighs she had wriggled impatiently, lifting her hips this way and that to make it easier for him to remove her briefs….

A sudden jolt flung Carrie into full consciousness. They had landed, she realised with surprise. Time to put her jacket on…gather her things. Would she ever escape Nico, waking or sleeping?

'You can let go of the arm rests now and relax,' the flight attendant told her with a smile.

If only it were that easy. 'Thank you for everything…'

The girl paused with her hand on the back of Carrie's seat. 'We'll be taxiing for around ten minutes before we reach the terminal building, so you'll have plenty of time to organise yourself. You'll have someone meeting you, I expect?'

No, no one. As loneliness washed over her Carrie realised why she had behaved the way she had on the night of the party.

She had wanted to be with someone who wanted her… And when that someone had been Nico… 'No, there's no one meeting me,' she admitted, spinning the words on a note of optimism. 'This is my first solo trip and I'm looking forward to it.'

'You know, I've always wanted to go it alone. I admire you.'

There was nothing to admire, Carrie thought, maintaining her upbeat expression. 'I'll let you know how it goes.'

As the flight attendant hurried away Carrie wondered if anything could blunt the passion she felt for Nico and allow her to think clearly. He didn't make it easy. 'Not yet, mouse, I set the pace…' That was what he had said to her at the party and she had been happy to fall into line. All that had to change now. No one challenged Nico, but she would now for the sake of their child.

It wasn't as if she was unprepared. She had played the scene where she told him about their baby over and over again in her head, preparing for rejection. She had even drafted the accusations for him: she should have been more responsible; she should have taken precautions; she should have been on the pill at the very least. Condoms? Condoms took a degree of forward thinking and there had been no time for that….

Freeing her seat belt and standing up, Carrie eased her way into the packed aisle. As she waited for the line to move forward a woman in front of her turned and said, 'Perfect, isn't it?'

Nico had said she was perfect….

No one had a door into her thoughts, Carrie told herself firmly. The woman was only making a comment about the sun-drenched landscape as they waited to disembark. 'Yes, perfect,' she agreed pleasantly, trying to blank the precise moment Nico had said that to her. But it was too late. She was already remembering Nico releasing the clasp on his jeans, lowering the zipper and freeing himself. Helping her to lift her legs and lock them around his waist, he'd leaned over her, pressed her knees back and said, 'Perfect…'

Her cheeks were on fire as she forced her thoughts back onto a practical track. It was important to keep her wits about her. She had nowhere to stay and very little money… So she would just have to take it one step at a time, Carrie reasoned calmly. First, she would find a bed for the night and then she would find Nico.

Doubt hit her again as she stepped onto the tarmac. As she looked around and inhaled the warm, spicy air she could tell that Niroli was even more glamorous and exclusive than she had thought. Even the airport officials were elegant. She felt pallid and shabby by comparison, just as she had on the night of the party….

Staring at her face in the bathroom mirror after they'd made love she had compared herself to the other women at the party and known she was plain. Her glorious hair was a bad joke that had landed on the wrong head. Just like one of the paper dolls she had played with as a child she was all jumbled up—the wrong eyes in the wrong face on the wrong body. It wasn't possible that Nico would want her for herself. Nico had wanted sex, and that was all. She had lost her virginity to a man who treated sex like a fast-food meal and used her like a disposable container.

And she was totally innocent of course, Carrie thought dryly, glancing up as she tried to orientate herself and search for some signs to Baggage Reclaim. She had encouraged Nico with everything she'd had, and, unsurprisingly, he had given in without a fight. The moment he had cupped her buttocks in his work-roughened hands was something she would never forget. She had rubbed herself against him, loving the sensation and knowing that for all his power in the boardroom Nico was a man who used physical strength as well as brainpower on-site. One of his greatest pleasures, he had confessed during a meeting where she had been taking notes, was to see his designs rise from the paper and take three-dimensional shape. He liked to see, touch, feel and suck everything he could out of each new experience.

She had always believed this thoroughness accounted for his success; she knew it made him a fantastic lover. She had been frantic by the time he had moved lightly back and forth and, when he had allowed the tip to catch inside her, it had shot the breath from her lungs like a punch. But he had pulled back before she'd had chance to close around him, by which time her body had been liquid fire. Working her nails cruelly into his bunched-up muscles, she had begged him, 'Nico, please…'

'Please, what?'

'You know what I want….'

'Do I?' He had seemed amused, and she'd gone way too far to pull back.

Face it, Carrie, you didn't want to pull back.

Carrie tried not to smile as she heaved her suitcase off the carousel, but it wasn't easy when she remembered the next time she had bucked towards him Nico had taken her deep.

Thinking about Nico was one way to get through the tedium of airport formalities, Carrie reflected, responding to a prompt to move forward in the queue. Handing over her passport, she smiled thinly in response to the immigration official's well-mannered scrutiny. Her mood had flattened, tiredness, maybe, or perhaps she had just reached the point in her reminiscences where it had all gone wrong. It had happened when Nico had said he loved her, because what he had actually said was, 'I love my mouse.' By reducing her to a cartoon image, Carrie guessed, Nico found it easier to brush her off. He didn't love

Carrie Evans, he loved the compliant mouse she had allowed him to think her.

Carrie's mood had deteriorated to the point where she was scanning the departure board for flights home by the time she'd walked across the concourse, but the moment she walked outside she changed her mind. Her artist's eye was immediately drawn to the richness and variety of the colours all around her. Fuchsia-tinted bougainvillea tumbled down yellow-sandstone walls and there was an imposing water feature in front of the terminal building throwing cascades of glittering spray into the air. Then she remembered Nico had designed the building and came back to earth with a bump.

What would he say when she told him about the baby?

What could he say?

Whatever happened she would never think of her baby as a mistake. Loving Nico was the only mistake she had made. Picking up her case, Carrie walked briskly towards the taxi rank.

The taxi driver, clearly proud of his beautiful island home, gave her a running commentary as he drove towards the old city of Niroli. The island had a colourful history, filled with ancient rivalries, rebels and kings. She learned that Nico's family's fortune had been founded on ancient trading routes, thanks to the island's tactically advantageous position to the south of Sicily.

Gradually Carrie found herself relaxing. The sky was so blue, and there wasn't a cloud in sight and everywhere she looked there was something new and interesting to see…ruined castles, vineyards, orange groves and fields and, leaning forward, she could see mountains capped with snow….

Niroli was beautiful, and it was easy for her to understand the elderly taxi driver's pride in his homeland. The only problem was his old taxi lacked air-conditioning and she was still wearing her heavy London suit. It was too late to wish she had been less impetuous and had thought to bring more clothes. When had she ever found calm reason possible where Nico was concerned?

Certainly not the morning after the party, Carrie thought as the taxi driver fell silent. She had taken such care with her appearance, knowing she was going to see Nico again. From her small stock of clothes she had chosen the best of her sombre suits and a sensible top. She hadn't wanted to look like a tease. She had felt shy and embarrassed, remembering her wantonness, her brazen pleading….

She had known it wasn't going to be easy to face him again, and the last thing she'd wanted was to give Nico the wrong idea. She had known the party was over.

But even so, deep inside she had harboured a kernel of hope… She had brushed her hair until it had gleamed, and had toyed with the idea of leaving it down, but as long hair was impractical in the office she had drawn it back before applying a touch of lipstick. She wasn't good at makeup, but she had made a special effort that day.

Her pulse had been off the scale, her body humming with awareness when she'd spotted Nico. He had been coming out of a breakfast meeting and she'd had to wait on tenterhooks for him to finish talking to a colleague. But then he'd walked past her….

'Good morning, Nico…'

She had to call again before he turned. And then his face had lit up, making her heart thunder.

'Oh, good, you're here.' He'd squeezed her arm and looked down into her eyes, all charm, all warmth…and well-honed professional courtesy. 'Scan these documents and get them back to me ASAP, will you, Carrie? We've got a rush on—' He'd pushed some papers into her hands, hands that had been holding him in the most intimate way only hours before. 'And could you bring some coffee to the boardroom?'

Sure of her answer, sure of her, he hadn't even bothered to turn around.

The boardroom had looked the same way it always did: stylish, clinical, perfect. Perfect for serious study and discussion, that was.

She'd done everything Nico'd asked of her that day and then she'd hung around after work like a kid with a crush. She'd waited until the office had emptied and the cleaners had arrived. Nico had still been at work in his office with the door closed. She'd had to do something, so she'd knocked on the door and poked her head round.

'Hi…'

He'd looked up, distracted. He'd had some plans in front of him and she could tell he hadn't want to be disturbed.

'Did you want something, Carrie?'

His eyes had been empty; they'd held nothing for her. Nico had been her boss and nothing more. The Nico she had encountered at the party might have been an imposter. To save face she'd told him a lie. 'Sorry to disturb you, Nico. I saw your light on and thought I'd pop by to see if you needed anything before I left.'

Dark eyes scanned her briefly. 'Nothing. Thank you, Carrie. You get home now. No need for you to stay late….'

The end.

It had come as swiftly and comprehensively as that.

It was over. As far as Nico had been concerned it had never begun. He'd seen no reason for them to feel awkward in the office. It was a one-off he had taken in his stride, and so should she. They had been hungry for sex and had gorged themselves on each other. No problem.

No problem… After that she couldn't remain working for him—her pride wouldn't allow her to. She loved him. She always would. And so she'd handed in her notice quietly like the mouse he'd thought her, making no fuss, simply saying that her aunt needed her to be at home.

The aftermath of her short-lived affair with Nico was more pain than Carrie cared to remember. She had been heartbroken and had cried herself to sleep each night, waking to each grey, unwanted day, still tired, still punishing herself for her foolishness. There had been no sunshine that summer, or if there had been she hadn't noticed it. All she remembered was the rain. It had rained and rained, matching her tear for tear as if she were engaged in some bizarre competition with the weather. And when she hadn't been crying she'd been raging at her stupidity, raging at the virginity she had thrown away on a man who didn't want her….

Until one day the sun had shone and she had sat up in bed and asked herself: was any man worth so much grief? That was the day she'd discovered she was pregnant with Nico's baby. She'd known then she had to wise up and toughen up. Ripping the blindfold off, she had accepted that Nico Fierezza had never pretended to be Mr Average, or Mr Comfort-Zone. Nico was a law unto himself and she had always known it. But she wasn't his mouse. She wasn't anybody's mouse. But she was going to be somebody's mother. And she was going to fight for that tiny soul for the rest of her life.

CHAPTER THREE

CARRIE settled into the quaint bed-and-breakfast in the centre of town, which the taxi driver had recommended. It wasn't far from the palace walls, and was everything he had promised her it would be: cheap, friendly and clean.

The excitement of being close to Nico kept her in a permanent state of agitation, which grew as she got ready to go out and explore for the first time. She might see him, she hoped from a distance to begin with, so she could feast her eyes and prepare for their meeting without complication.

Like everyone else at the office she had wondered about Nico's private life. He didn't have a wife, so, did he have a mistress? Surely, there was someone? What did Nico Fierezza do to amuse himself when he wasn't courting danger, or at work? Carrie had always felt uncomfortable when she had heard her colleagues discussing him. It had made her feel protective towards him. She had wanted to tell them to leave him alone, but that would have given away her true feelings. She knew why they were fascinated. Nico's restlessness made women want to tie him down. He pursued danger and they pursued him. Nico lived his life on the edge, and they wanted to be part of it. By not putting himself in the way of gossip he had only succeeded in making himself more talked about, more desired. He gave the impression of a man searching for something just outside his reach. Women knew this and it made him irresistible; it made them long to be his final destination.

She paused to search the street as she left the hotel. Searching for Nico had become a reflex action… And one she had to snap out of, Carrie told herself firmly. But soon her mood lifted. It was hard not to smile when the weather was so beautiful and the people were so friendly. She had barely taken a dozen steps before someone greeted her with a smile.

That was what living in a warm country did for you, Carrie reflected. People came out of their shell as if they wanted you to share in their good fortune at living in such a lovely country. And Niroli was beautiful. She could understand that Nico might want to stay here for ever, though her heart squeezed tight at the thought of it. She had to remind herself that her priority now was a change of clothes. Her budget was tight, but she could afford a simple summer dress and a pair of sandals.

The winding streets lined with boutiques invited investigation and, as Carrie turned onto one offering tempting views of the harbour, she imagined what it might have been like to have discovered it with Nico. Steeply banked steps lined with iron handrails led down to the sea, and she could picture them running hand in hand… Nico steadying her and both of them laughing beneath the strings of brightly coloured washing…

But that was just a foolish fantasy, and exploring had to wait for another day. She had to buy something cool to wear, or she would melt.

She stepped out of the sunlight into the fridge-like temperature of a small boutique. A bell rang deep in the interior of the shop and she could hear a woman talking in an imperious voice somewhere out of sight.

Everyone would be attending to her, Carrie reasoned, taking care not to touch any of the expensive clothes. She realised she must have strayed into one of the most exclusive designer boutiques on the island, and didn't need to look at the price tags to know there was nothing here she could afford. But she could hardly walk out. The best thing was to wait and ask one of the assistants for directions to the nearest high street store.

Carrie pressed back, making herself invisible as a customer appeared in a flurry of self-importance. The older woman was tall and svelte, and a group of young women rushed in her wake, each of them carrying an elaborate evening gown cloaked in a transparent protective cover. A sleek black limousine swept up to the kerb right on cue, and a chauffeur in full uniform leapt out. Opening the rear door with a flourish, he bowed low as he waited for his elegant passenger to step inside. Once settled, the woman dismissed him with a flick of her wrist.

Carrie was fascinated and, as the limousine swept away and the street fell silent again, she knew it only reinforced her impression that the island Nico called home was out of her league. What more surprises lurked behind the island's beautiful face?

'And that was just the *principessa's* lady-in-waiting…'

As the young assistant burst through the door Carrie had to laugh as the young girl made a fanning motion in front of her mouth as if her fingers were on fire.

'I'm sorry to keep you waiting, *signorina,*' she said, still smiling at Carrie. 'Can I help you?'

Seeing herself in one of the mirrors, Carrie lost confidence for a moment. Even after straightening herself out at the hotel, by comparison with the young shop assistant she looked unfashionably dull. 'I was hoping you could tell me where to find the nearest department store?'

'A department store in Niroli?' The girl quickly hid her amazement. 'We don't have one, *signorina*. But we do have a lovely market,' she added, 'and that's just down the street. There are some very good clothing stalls on the market. I use them myself. Would you like me to show you?'

Warming to the young girl's friendliness, Carrie found it went a long way to restoring her self-confidence and allowed her to ask the question she was dying to ask. 'When you said that was just the *principessa's* lady-in-waiting, to whom were you referring?'

'To *Principessa* Anastasia.' The girl pulled a face. 'The woman you saw was the Contessa di Palesi.' She pulled an even bigger face. 'They are staying at the palace and the *contessa* is the *principessa's* principal lady-in-waiting.'

As the girl continued to grimace comically Carrie forced a laugh, but inside she was in pieces. She had always known it would turn out like this and that Nico would choose someone from his own class, but having her worst fears confirmed made her heart clench tight. She hated the thought of a princess staying at the palace with Nico, but as there was no hiding from the truth and she was curious… 'Why was the *contessa* so angry?'

'Because there is an important dinner at the palace tonight and the *principessa's* gown is missing a button.' The girl shrugged. 'She won't wear it, of course. Not even if we sew it on again. "How can the *principessa* wear damaged goods?"' The young girl started to giggle after doing a good impression of the *contessa's* voice. 'And so we have provided the *principessa* with a selection of gowns to choose from.'

Carrie could only wonder at the sort of wealth that allowed someone to discard a dress merely because it was missing a button, and the girl's phrase 'damaged goods' rang in her ears. Would that be how Nico saw her now?

Carrie forced her thoughts onto another, more practical course. 'Do you think I'll be able to buy a summer dress and some sandals at the market?'

'*Certo*,' the young girl replied, smiling encouragement. 'There is a lovely stall where I buy such things, myself. You will find it just beneath the walls of the palace. Here, let me show you. Can you see it?'

Carrie's pulse picked up pace as she stared at the palace. She already knew that the ancient building was much bigger and far more impressive than the photographs in the in-flight magazine had suggested. Even from her bedroom window at the top of the hotel she had to crane her neck to see the pennants flying on the battlements. Pennants she knew now must be flying in honour of Princess Anastasia. It didn't take much to imagine what a prominent member of another European royal family was doing at the palace with Nico, or why there was an important dinner tonight... Could she have chosen a worse time to deliver her news? Nico was rich in his own right, he was highly successful and well respected, plus he was the grandson of a king. Why else would Princess Anastasia be staying at the palace if not to announce their betrothal?

Carrie hid her anxiety as she said goodbye to the young shop assistant, but she was racked by the knowledge that, although she carried Nico's child, unlike Princess Anastasia she was firmly locked out on the wrong side of the palace walls.

It was while she was walking towards the market that Carrie saw a notice advertising a tour of the old city that took in part of the palace.

If she could get inside...

Even as her spirits soared a wave of nausea swept over her, reminding her to take cover from the sun and buy some water.

The heat was relentless and the physical effects of her pregnancy could often steal her strength away like this.

Having bought the water, she drank it down and was just leaving the shop when the footpath across the street erupted into noisy mayhem. A storm of paparazzi appeared out of nowhere and, for a few moments, there was nothing but noise and confusion and flashlights going off.

It was Nico. Carrie held her breath; every part of her body had tensed. She didn't need to see him to know he was there; she could feel him in every fibre of her being. And now she could see him… At least a head taller than the other men and so commanding that even the scurrying photographers had backed away to snatch their shots from a safe distance…

As if Nico would lash out at them, Carrie thought, angry on his behalf. He was a man, they were boys; what did they know?

The surge of love she felt put her back where she'd always been, stunned by Nico's presence, by his aura, his physique. Nico Fierezza was one of the most eligible men in the world and he was also one of the most attractive. She didn't need media photographs to know he had the face of a film star and the body of a bare-knuckled fighter. And Nico had wanted her. Nico had wanted Carrie Evans, a pallid pudding, with nothing more to recommend her than a hundred-words-a-minute typing speed. And now he was the father of her child….

Even as pride swelled inside her Carrie noticed the woman at Nico's side, the woman he was protecting from the photographers. She was young and very beautiful… Could this be Anastasia?

Carrie couldn't tear her gaze away from a girl so lovely she was like a princess in a fairy tale. A princess who was everything she was not. Elegant and cool, she had glossy black hair that hung like a curtain down her back, caressing her naked shoulders like a silken cape. Every inch of her was tanned a deep golden brown and her skin was smooth and flawless. Her lips were red and full and, though her eyes were hidden behind the latest designer sunglasses, her teeth were film star perfect as she smiled up at Nico.

Carrie couldn't see Nico's expression, but she was sure that he was smiling, too.

Why was she surprised? She had always known Nico would have a beautiful woman by his side. She had always known her one night with him was more than she deserved. It was time for her to accept that when Nico had withdrawn carefully, pulling down her skirt, and settling her on her feet, he had withdrawn from her in every way a man could withdraw from a woman….

She shrank deeper into the shadows as Nico threw a stare her way. Had he sensed her presence?

Taking no chances, Carrie pressed back against the cold stone wall. It was then that she saw the bodyguards tailing Nico and the princess to their car.

Her instincts had saved her this time, but she would have to be more careful in future. Being taken into custody in front of her baby's father wasn't quite what she had in mind!

CHAPTER FOUR

CARRIE found she was trembling as Nico and Anastasia drove away. It didn't matter how many times she told herself there must be a woman in Nico's life, seeing him with someone was more than she could bear. The blacked-out windows of his high-performance car hinted at intimate spaces and close personal contact. How could he fail to touch the princess as he leaned across? How could the princess fail to be intoxicated by Nico's cologne, or by his clean, warm scent? Princess Anastasia was beautiful, and Nico… Nico was Nico. How could they resist each other? She had seen the way the princess looked at him.

But it was more than physical contact that she resented, much more. It was the intimacy of shared conversation and getting to know each other that tore at her heart. But she had to face facts. She didn't stand a chance with Nico, she never had. And if he hadn't wanted her three months ago he would hardly want her now. And when she told him about the baby… What would he think when he compared the mother of his child to Princess Anastasia?

By the time she had dredged up every negative thought and examined it twice, Carrie was close to tears. But as crying wouldn't get her anywhere she pulled out her purse and paid the stallholder for a simple summer dress and a pair of plastic flip-flops instead.

Wasn't that the perfect outfit for her meeting with Nico at the palace? Carrie reflected wryly. On impulse she added some new underwear to her purchases. Why not? No one would see the frivolous garments, but she would know they were there. It was a small defiance, but sometimes she found small things the most effective.

Having showered and changed into her new outfit, Carrie splashed cold water onto her face and then tied her hair back. By the time she left the guest-house the temperature was soaring and even the stone beneath her feet seemed to radiate heat, which didn't bode well for her plastic sandals.

She hadn't realised how far she would have to walk, or that it would all be uphill. She hadn't thought about the shops closing in the afternoon, or the fact that they wouldn't open again until seven that same evening. And she had forgotten her sunglasses and her sun lotion in her rush to fly to Niroli. In fact, she had forgotten all the essentials. It was unlike her to be so reckless and impetuous, but her life had never collided with Nico's before.

Turning the corner, she frowned with concern seeing how many people were waiting to take the tour of the old city. The queue snaked round another corner out of sight, and she was already exhausted, plus she had developed blisters between her toes where the plastic thong of the flip-flops had rubbed her. Looking down, she saw her feet were bleeding.

Pausing in the shade next to one of the palace control posts, Carrie watched the vehicles driving in and out. There was a guard seated behind a glass window in a small command station, and the palace courtyard was just a tantalising few steps away… Going up to the window, she tapped on it politely.

Thanks to the young shop assistant she knew all about the state banquet, and when the officer looked up she told him that she was one of the casual staff hired for that evening to work in the kitchen.

Consulting his list, the officer shook his head.

'I'm not there?' Carrie pretended dismay. 'But I must be…they're expecting me.'

'This is the wrong entrance,' the man told her. 'Waiting staff must go round the back.' He tipped his chin.

'What if they don't have my name there, either?' Carrie pressed, adding a plaintive note to her voice. Maybe she reminded the guard of his sister, or some other female he knew, because to her relief the guard's manner changed towards her.

'All right.' He gave her a reassuring wink. 'I'll call them and tell them to expect you.'

'Oh, would you? That's really kind of you. Thank you so much.' She dropped her gaze and assumed a meek expression, waiting on tenterhooks for the guard to lift his receiver and speak to his opposite number on the other gate.

Without looking at her he waved her on….

She was inside the palace! Steeling herself to inquisitive eyes, Carrie walked quickly through the servants' door, her heart thundering with apprehension.

'*La cucina?*' she said when anyone stared directly at her. Her knowledge of Italian was limited to the name of the Italian restaurant close to her aunt's house, which fortunately had been called La Cucina Italia, or The Italian Kitchen.

Everyone was in such a hurry to get to their appointed place no one thought to question her, or notice when she slipped away. Darting up a stone staircase, Carrie had no idea where she was heading, only that reason told her the private apartments of the royal family would be above the servants' quarters.

This was madness, she decided, pausing on the stairwell to shed her shoes. She would have to chance her luck and take the next door she found….

Stepping cautiously through an arched doorway, Carrie lingered a moment on the plush carpet to get her bearings. She was in a long and splendid corridor where grizzled Fierezza ancestors stared down sternly from the walls. There was a faint aroma of beeswax and lavender and hangings were ruby-coloured silk…

This was Nico's home, Carrie reminded herself, shivering as she looked around. It was imperial splendour on the grandest scale, but it was cold and unwelcoming… But Nico was here somewhere, and now all she had to do was find him.

He had to get some air. The artificial atmosphere in the air-conditioned palace was getting to him. But above that, he was in a mood so black he wouldn't inflict it on anyone, not even his grandfather the king, who was largely responsible for it.

King Giorgio was ninety years old, a fact Nico couldn't ignore. It was the only reason he hadn't made his views clear in his usual blunt fashion. His grandfather had proved himself shrewd enough and hard enough to hold the throne and guide Niroli into the twenty-first century, but that didn't give him licence to construct a future for his heirs. Nico was prepared to accommodate reasonable requests, but he would not allow his grandfather to direct his life….

Increasing the pace of his stride, he took a short cut through the covered walkway leading to the private apartments. He grew angrier as he reviewed his conversation with the king.

His grandfather had offered him the kingdom of Niroli as if it were the winning ticket in a lottery. Nico Fierezza, King of Niroli? He had never heard anything so ridiculous in his life. The idea of living at court had never appealed to him. He would rather take a swim in a sea of sharks than become the ruler of a kingdom surrounded by sycophants.

His grandfather's offer had only proved the king didn't know him at all. What was he supposed to do? Land on the island, grab a crown and cheer? He had a life and people who depended on him away from Niroli. There wasn't a chance he was going to leave the team who worked with him in the lurch in order to accept the crown.

But his grandfather was old and ailing, and he couldn't turn his dearest wish down flat. And so he had agreed to withhold his final answer for a day or two, though his decision was already made. He would find a way to break the news gently to his grandfather in spite of the fact that delay went against everything he believed in.

And then there was the Princess Anastasia, the lure by which his grandfather had thought to tempt him to take the throne. She was beautiful enough, but not for him. Nico preferred his women without adornment, and his sense of humour had suffered a severe malfunction when he had found himself tricked into a lunch date with the overdressed princess. As gaudy as the pennants flying in her honour, Princess Anastasia was about as subtle in her intentions towards him as a bitch in heat.

And now there was a state dinner to sit through, which was also being held in her honour. To soften the harder blow yet to come he had agreed with his grandfather that he would partner the princess, and she was waiting for him now, no doubt sporting half a ton of diamonds.

He wasn't exactly dressed down, himself, Nico conceded, easing his neck beneath the stiff winged collar. A state dinner required him to wear full regalia, and so he was wearing the official uniform he kept at the palace, complete with the sash that marked him out as a grandson of the king. The formality irked him, but it wouldn't hurt him to follow tradition for one night.

And he could hardly wear jeans…

Nico's lips curved briefly in amusement, but quickly flattened again. He had just entered the courtyard leading to the guest suite where Princess Anastasia was staying when he spotted the intruder. Some ragamuffin was sitting on the lip of the fountain dabbling her feet in the pool. 'This area is closed to the public—' He froze as she turned around.

'Carrie…' The shock hit him like a blow in the chest. What was his secretary doing here? 'Carrie? Answer me.' He was beginning to feel irritated. He hadn't seen her for… how long? And she just turned up like this? Where had she been? What had happened to her? She had disappeared with no explanation at all. She hadn't warned him, or worked her notice, or even troubled to send him a letter of resignation. Everyone in the office had missed her. He'd missed her. 'Carrie, speak to me…'

As she stared at him events played fast forward behind his eyes. The night of the party…the devil on his back…his frustration at being forced to stand around making small talk…his gaze settling on Carrie…seeing her looking as uncomfortable as he felt and not half as good as he was at hiding it… He'd wanted to save her embarrassment and had ended up giving way to an urge that had been nagging at him since the first day they'd met. And he'd been surprised by her response— make that amazed. He'd always thought her a mouse, maybe because she had been such a calming influence in the office, going quietly about her duties, making no fuss. He had appreciated her for those very qualities, but that night had completely changed his perception of her.

'Carrie, what's wrong with you? Answer me...' A rush of concern propelled him towards her, but then caution held him back. She looked tired, but today he was a prince and this was Niroli, and Carrie Evans was his secretary, or she had been once.

'Why are you here?' His surprise was replaced by suspicion as he ran through the possibilities in his mind. She'd come a long way to find him. Why? He'd never made her any promises. They'd been together one time, and that had been for sex. They both knew it. It could never be anything more and she'd been fine with it at the time.

She couldn't breathe. Had she really imagined she was ready for this? The passion in Nico's eyes reminded her of hot, steamy sex; he'd worn that same fierce, intent look then. She found him doubly intimidating dressed as a prince...doubly attractive because he was fresh from the shower, his hair still damply curling, his face already starting to darken with stubble. His cheekbones appeared carved in flint above his unforgiving mouth. How she longed to soften it....

'Why are you here, Carrie?' he repeated.

'I came to see you, Nico.' Planting her hands on the cold stone behind her she braced herself for disappointment.

'You look exhausted.'

The concern growing in his eyes made something catch in her heart. 'I have to talk to you... Could we go somewhere else?' She glanced around the courtyard.

'Why not here?'

'Because I'd like to speak to you in private.'

Suspicion replaced the concern in his eyes. Nico's reading of the situation was making her nervous. And then he glanced at his watch, a clear indication that he had somewhere else to be.

'I can give you about ten minutes,' he said.

Ten minutes…

Nico's apartment at the palace was like nothing Carrie had ever seen before, not even in magazines. It was exquisite, delicate, refined and restrained. Classical music played softly in the background and candles flickered in silver sconces.

'Well?' he said, but she could see he was itching to get away and she needed his full attention.

He had to distance himself from her…he had to put physical distance between them so he couldn't inhale her fragrant scent or feel the warmth of her body reaching out to him. Seeing her again had affected him far more than he had expected. What was it about the woman? She wasn't beautiful. She had no skill at repartee. But even that made him smile, for he wasn't noted for his small talk, either. She had a fabulous figure and glorious hair, but other than that she was plain. Even so, she touched him in some way he couldn't name. She tempered him. Except in one way, of course… 'Come on, Carrie,' he prompted, conscious of time slipping by.

Nico was staying as far away from her as possible. She remained by the door wishing she hadn't been so naïve, hadn't misread the situation so badly. She could have sent him a solicitor's letter, but now she was here she had to go through with it.

She walked deeper into the room and stopped just in front of him. He stiffened as if wondering what she was going to do next, and then a look she knew well came into his eyes.

'Oh, I see,' he murmured.

And then she was enfolded in his scent, in his warmth, in the sheer power of him, and all of it so blessedly familiar. He didn't give her chance to speak or to breathe before teasing her lips with his tongue and his teeth, urging her in a low, rough voice to do all manner of wicked things. Parting her lips she drank him in, and was already scrambling up him by the time he backed her towards the wall. After vowing to resist him she was forced to accept there were some things reason had no power over, and this was one of them.

Her briefs came down in the same moment Nico freed himself. He paused briefly to make some comment about the sexy red lace. She only caught a glimpse of him, but it was enough to know he was engorged and magnificent. And she was ready. Cupping her buttocks, he helped her to lock her legs around his waist, and then thrust deep. Holding her weight as if it were nothing he forced her back against the wall, working efficiently, pounding rhythmically until she came, which was almost at once. She cried out so loud he was forced to put a hand over her mouth in case the servants heard her. Only Nico brought out this wild side in her nature and she bit him for his trouble. Snatching his hand away, he stared at it, looking in amazement at the teeth marks she had left. And then he laughed.

She laughed, too…softly, intimately, relishing the shared moment until he grew serious and, holding her gaze, very deliberately sank into her again.

It was more pleasure than she had ever known. Throwing back her head, she dragged in air. Nico was calmer and more controlled now and took his time.

'Was that good?' He eased out of her.

Good…

But moments after lowering her to her feet, he added, 'Was that what you came for, Carrie?'

The remark was like a dash of cold water in her face. How could she have forgotten why she was here?

'I take it that is why you came to Niroli?' His lips tugged up in a cynical smile and he eased his shoulders as if he'd had a good workout. 'You can use the bathroom off the corridor while I take a quick shower. When you've finished I'll have someone show you out…'

The way she felt…failure didn't even begin to cover it. She walked numbly in the direction he indicated and then stopped by the door, lacking the will to move until Nico left the room.

He paced up and down outside the bathroom door waiting for her to come out. What was keeping her?

He stepped back as she opened the door. She looked like a wraith. What had happened to Carrie since she had left the office? And what was coming next? He couldn't help remembering her raunchy underwear. There was a whole lot more to this woman he wasn't getting.

She glanced up and blushed as if she sensed his mood deteriorating. She was right to be worried. How she could she be so sexually charged one moment and so meek and mild the next? It was enough to make any man suspicious.

But then she stumbled, and he caught her, and when he had to hold her close he felt things he didn't want to feel. He'd fought emotion all his life. He reacted the usual way, with swift rejection of his feelings. 'What's happened to you, Carrie?'

'You happened to me, Nico…' She quickly recovered and, straightening up, brushed away his steadying hand. 'You're like a drug… A drug I find dangerously addictive.'

It was such a piece of drama coming from his mouse he almost laughed. They both knew what they had, and that it wasn't going anywhere. It was then he saw her feet were bleeding. 'For goodness' sake, Carrie, why didn't you say something?'

He hadn't meant to sound so harsh and felt bad seeing tears in her eyes. They were such tiny feet, on closer inspection, and the damage had been done by some cheap plastic sandals. He felt a tug somewhere deep inside him, which he immediately shrugged off. 'We'll have to do something about this,' he said impatiently, glancing at his watch.

The small first-aid room was located just off the palace kitchen. It was tiled in white and smelled of disinfectant. Carrie couldn't care less about her feet. She was with Nico and now she had to tell him her news.

He ran some warm water into a bowl, and added a drop of disinfectant. Grabbing a towel, he swung it over his shoulder. 'Put your feet in here. You'll have to soak them for a few minutes.'

Remembering his ten-minute deadline, Carrie felt hysterical laughter leap in her throat. But she didn't see the funny side for long. His deadline undoubtedly involved Princess Anastasia. Nico could look forward to his evening with the princess now that he was replete and could relax. He might come from the highest family in the land, but Nico was a primal force who needed a regular outlet for his energy, and she was that outlet when there was no other sport to be enjoyed. Taking her up against the wall when the servants might have come in at any moment and disturbed them was just another form of risk-taking, providing Nico with all the elements of danger he enjoyed.

She had enjoyed it, too, Carrie accepted. More than enjoyed it. Nico's love-making filled her with joy and with purpose…while it lasted. But lust was no foundation for a family, and maybe she could bear the pain of his rejection, but she didn't want that for her baby.

When Nico examined her feet and handled them with the greatest care it was all she could do to hold back her tears. All she had ever wanted was a home full of love, a family, and she wanted Nico to be part of that family.

'How could you do this to yourself, Carrie?' he demanded reproachfully.

'I didn't do it on purpose.' She kept her voice light. She didn't want Nico to feel responsible for her. She didn't want him thinking her weak; he must never think her weak. She wasn't his mouse, and never would be again, not now that she had a child to consider.

'These shoes are meant for the beach, not for walking round town.'

'I only had city shoes with me when I landed, and I couldn't find any shops—'

'There are plenty of shops…'

But none she could afford, Carrie thought, not wanting to say as much to Nico. She didn't want to give him the impression that she was hard up, or a hard-luck case.

He looked at her thoughtfully, as if he knew she couldn't afford anything from the shops in Niroli, and maybe even admired her a little for keeping silent.

She hoped that was what had brought the softening to his lips. 'I should have known I can't wear flip-flops; they always hurt my feet.'

'If you knew—' He stopped as if he didn't want to start an argument and started storming through the cupboards instead. 'There should be antiseptic cream in here somewhere….'

He insisted on drying her feet on a fluffy white towel,

which he rested on his knees. And when he put the cream on he did so very gently.

She had to brace herself. She had to tense every muscle so she didn't show him how that made her feel, but even so her eyes filled with tears.

'It isn't that bad, is it?' Nico said, straightening up to look at her.

Worse than he knew. 'No, fine,' she assured him.

And then he did the one thing she dreaded most. Reaching into the inside breast pocket of his jacket, he pulled out a wad of notes. 'You really must get yourself some decent shoes, Carrie.'

She could only stare in horror at the money.

'Here, take it,' he pressed.

'I don't want it…' She couldn't stop staring at it.

'Don't be so silly,' he insisted. 'You used to work for me. Let's call it severance pay, if that makes you feel better.'

'Let's not…' Firming her lips, she slipped down from the seat. 'Will you show me out, or shall I find someone else to do it?'

He moved in front of the door to block her way. 'What's wrong with you, Carrie? You never used to be like this—'

'You mean I used to be a pushover?'

'No, I don't mean that, and you know it—'

'Do I, Nico?' She was conscious that the mood had disintegrated into acrimony. How could she tell him about their baby now? She was determined to choose the right moment, and this wasn't it. 'Thank you for bathing my feet.' She glanced at the door.

'You're not leaving until you tell me why you're here.'

'Then we're going to be here a very long time.'

'I need an answer, Carrie.'

'Aren't you going to be late for the princess?'

'She can wait.'

Nico's attitude surprised her. It suggested he was in no hurry to see Anastasia. Or was that just wishful thinking on her part?

He glanced at his watch again. 'We'll have to make another appointment. I can't do this now…'

Carrie's cheeks blazed red. No doubt a regular meeting while she was on the island would be convenient for Nico.

'You want something from me,' he said, fixing her with a firm stare, 'and I'm going to find out what it is.'

'Yes, I do want something,' Carrie admitted, 'but it's not what you think—'

'All right, I'll make time. We'll discuss it now.'

'And make you late for the state banquet?'

'Like the princess, that can wait.'

CHAPTER FIVE

CLOSING the door to his private apartment, Nico watched as Carrie took in her surroundings. She had liked it the first time, and now she wanted to have a closer look at things. Many of the pieces he kept in Niroli belonged in a museum, but he had grown up with them. That was the trouble with extreme wealth—you took everything for granted—and he hardly noticed the trappings now. But seeing the room through Carrie's eyes made him appreciate things he'd hardly noticed before.

She was impressed, though not by the value of his possessions, she was genuinely interested. He watched her dip her head to examine a jade ornament more closely.

'Do you like it?' She was trailing her forefinger across the back of a Ming-dynasty horse. It was priceless, but, of course, she couldn't know that. It had a finely carved saddle with elaborate fringing, and was an outstanding example of some ancient artisan's skill. There was no chance he could give it to her, but he'd seen pictures of it in the palace gift store. 'I'm sure we can find you a postcard in the shop.'

The look she gave him was pure ice. A postcard in exchange for sex—was that what she thought? He brought the shutters down. He couldn't risk antagonising her until he found out what she was doing in Niroli.

* * *

She didn't want a trip to the gift shop as a reward for being a good girl, and she felt like telling Nico to get over himself. She wanted to tell him that his fabulous wealth would pale in the face of her news, but when he eased his collar and moved restlessly she knew he was uncomfortable in a room with overdressed windows and silk-draped walls, and felt some sympathy for him. Her first impression of the décor had been good, but on closer inspection Carrie thought it cloying and could see why it wouldn't suit Nico. The palace might be his family home, but Nico was a free spirit. Niroli was too small an island to contain him, and his decision to leave the country as a youth to make his way in London was certainly no mystery to her now. She was beginning to understand him, which gave her courage. 'This isn't easy for me, Nico…'

'Try me,' he prompted.

'When I left the office, I had no idea that…' He nodded encouragement. 'I had no idea that I was pregnant.'

'What?'

He sounded and looked incredulous. 'I'm pregnant,' she said again, telling him the news in a soft, happy voice. The idea was still new to her, still surrounded by its own little aura of light.

It took her a moment to realise how quiet the room had become, and then Nico said evenly, 'What's that got to do with me?'

Her tongue froze, and at the very moment when she should have been at her most eloquent she saw his mouth begin to curve with contempt. 'E-everything,' she managed to stutter, feeling in that moment as if she had been sucked into outer space where there was no warmth, no air, no comfort for her anywhere.

'What do you mean, Carrie? "Everything?"'

'I mean, you're the father of my baby, Nico—'

'What?' he exploded. His voice had gone instantly cold and, shaking his head, he turned away.

'Nico, I swear—'

'You swear?' He turned back, head down, eyes full of a terrifying emotion she'd never seen before. She reached out to him, but he pulled away.

She was a liar. *Carrie was a liar.* She had reminded him in the cruellest way possible that he was infertile and could never have the family he longed for. Emotion swirled inside him, threatening to erupt. It escaped in words, harsh, ugly words: 'I'm not the father of your baby, Carrie.'

He wasn't prepared for the pain he felt saying that—the pain of knowing the child she carried couldn't be his. It was unbearable, excruciating; he couldn't bear to think of her with some other man. 'We had sex,' he said cruelly, instinct driving him to hurt as much as she had hurt him. 'We had sex, and that was all—'

'It wasn't just sex to me, Nico.'

How could she think him so gullible? She asked too much. The travesty of wanting something so badly only to have it delivered to him twisted and spoiled…'If it wasn't sex what was it?' The ferocity in his voice shocked him and he didn't know if he could control the rage building inside him. If he couldn't then he must end this now. 'Did you think I would go down on bended knee the next morning and propose marriage to you?' His eyes, his voice couldn't have been harder.

'Please, Nico—'

'Don't touch me!' He shook her off. 'You wanted sex every bit as much as I did and we both knew what we were doing. You hadn't been drinking; I'd been watching you, so don't go down that road. Sex that night had nothing to do with love, or long-term commitment, and I never let you think that once, did I?'

She couldn't argue with him. She was too stunned, too sick inside to know how to answer him.

'I'll write you a cheque now if that's what it takes to get you off my back.'

Nico's cruel words forced Carrie to face the truth. Her child had been conceived in a ferment of lust, and her baby's father couldn't stand the sight of her. But she loved him. She still loved him. She always would.

'Let's stop playing games, Carrie.'

Something was nagging at her, something wasn't right. Nico was so sure of himself, so very sure…

'I don't know who you've been with, or why he won't support you, but if you've come here out of desperation just tell me how much you want.'

Carrie was stunned. She couldn't believe what Nico was thinking. 'I don't want your money.'

'Then, what do you want?'

'I want nothing for myself. All I ask is that you acknowledge our child—'

'*Our* child? I don't have a child! And as for you?' His stare lingered on her still-flat stomach. 'How do I know you're even pregnant?' His gaze flashed up, demanding an answer.

'Do you think I'd lie about something like this?'

'How do I know what to think? You sneak into the palace like a thief—'

'Don't turn this into something squalid!'

'Don't you!' Nico warned softly. 'The Carrie Evans I knew wouldn't use a child as a bargaining counter.'

'And I'm not doing that now. Nico, how can you be so sure you're not the father of my child?'

'I know I'm not.' His mouth flattened, telling her that was his final answer.

'But there's been no one else,' Carrie said in confusion. 'The baby is yours—'

'No one else?' Nico cut across her.

His silence now reminded Carrie of the frivolous underwear she had bought on the market, the underwear she had helped him to remove. Surely, he didn't think… 'Nico, please believe me, I was a virgin that night—'

'A virgin?' He shook his head grimly. 'This lie of yours has gone far enough.' Taking hold of her, he tried to lead her from the room, but she had more strength than he knew.

'I suggest you leave before I do something I might regret, Carrie.'

'Like what?' She refused to move another inch. 'What would you do, Nico? Would you hit me? Would you force me out of here? Would you strike a pregnant woman?'

The blood drained from his face. 'I wouldn't touch anyone in mindless anger.'

'Just as I wouldn't lie to you,' she assured him, holding his gaze, willing him to believe her.

'You've just proved that you would,' Nico said. Walking to the door, he opened it wide. 'Now, please leave.'

'Nico—'

He turned his face away from her as if he couldn't bear the sight of her a moment longer and his voice when he spoke next was the voice of a stranger. 'I feel as if I've been with a very different woman to the sweet girl I employed. You're a better actress than I thought, Carrie Evans, and a crueller one, but don't think you can lay your mistakes at my door.'

'My baby isn't a mistake,' she assured him tensely. 'The only mistake I made was getting involved with you.'

'It's time to accept I'm not the father of your baby.'

'Nico, you must believe—'.

'I can assure you I'm not. Your plan has badly misfired.'

'My plan?' She looked at him in bewilderment, but there was no chance to press him because in her worst nightmare come true Princess Anastasia was bearing down on them.

Wearing a slinky black dress with earrings so long the diamonds glittered on her shoulders like drops of sweat, the princess came straight to Nico's side and linked arms with him.

'Darling, what's taking you so long?' she purred into his ear.

'Forgive me, Anastasia,' he said smoothly, moving away. Thrusting Carrie behind him, Nico planted himself in front of her.

Carrie blenched as she viewed her rival through the small space left between Nico and the door frame. She might as well retire gracefully now. She was nothing but a little drab compared to the princess.

'I heard raised voices, darling.' Peering round Nico, Anastasia tried to get a better view of Carrie. 'You don't have a problem, I hope?'

'No problem,' Nico said evenly.

For a moment Carrie was surprised that Nico was troubling to protect her, but then she realised he was protecting his flawless reputation. Nico was used to sailing above the trivial embarrassments that afflicted the rest of mankind, and she guessed finding himself on the back foot was something new for him.

'*Is* there a problem, Nico?' Anastasia pressed. 'They told me you had been detained.' She gave a pretty pout. 'But they also promised me that you would be joining us for coffee… Is this girl bothering you?' Craning her elegant neck, she stared down her perfect ski-slope nose at Carrie.

Nico stood to one side, leaving the two women in full sight of each other. 'Carrie Evans used to work for me.'

'I see…' Finely plucked eyebrows soared at an acute angle as the princess evaluated her opponent.

'Carrie's in Niroli on holiday, aren't you, Carrie?'

Nico was prompting her? Carrie chose to remain silent.

'Carrie, may I present Princess Anastasia….'

As Nico introduced her to the princess she stood stiffly, hoping Anastasia didn't expect her to curtsy; the princess's haughty gaze had instantly labelled her an inferior.

'Why, Anastasia…nothing to say?' Nico pressed. 'Is there a reason Ms Evans shouldn't visit the palace while she's holidaying in Niroli?' His voice was like a velvet threat, and as he spoke a quiver of response ran across Carrie's shoulders.

'No reason at all,' Princess Anastasia said quickly, opening her eyes very wide to signal her absolute agreement with anything Nico chose to say about the matter.

He was playing them off against each other, Carrie realised. This might be providing Nico with an amusing interlude, but she wasn't going to play. On the other hand, who knew what lengths Anastasia would go to in order to ingratiate herself with Nico? Any and all, Carrie concluded, watching the princess moisten her lips with the tip of her tongue.

'I hope you will accept my apologies, *Principessa?*'

As Nico spoke Carrie had to hide her feelings, for, overriding the desire to scratch out Anastasia's eyes was the desire to laugh. The role of penitent was completely beyond Nico's acting capabilities. The princess didn't seem to realise this and her soft exhalation of breath assured Carrie that Anastasia would take Nico on any terms.

'I do hope we're not too late for the last dance?' Nico added, bowing low to Anastasia.

As his sardonic glance brushed her face Carrie knew she had been relegated to the position of silent servant. Nico and his princess were conducting a conversation that excluded her. Could he have found a crueller way to put her in her place?

'Of course we're not too late for the last dance, *caro,*' Anastasia assured him, and this time she did include Carrie in the conversation, if only to shoot her a look of triumph.

'Shall we go?' Nico offered with yet another bow.

How charming he could be when it suited him, Carrie thought, narrowing her eyes as Nico deigned to acknowledge her with a slight tilt of his head.

'I'll have one of the palace drivers take you back to your hotel,' he said to her, pausing mid-stride as if she were an afterthought. 'Wait in the courtyard and I'll have them come and find you—'

'I can make my own way back to the hotel, thank you,' she told him with composure.

Carrie's defiant pose lasted only until the regal pair was out of sight. To hear them chatting so easily together was sheer torture. She was forced to admit they did look stunning together, but as Anastasia's laugh rang out she thought again that Nico had it all. Having enjoyed his entertainment on the side he could relax and escort his beautiful princess to the ball. While she remained in the shadows listening to the rustle of Anastasia's silk gown brush against the wall like a mocking reproach.

Carrie waited until she was sure the coast was clear and then hurried in the same direction as Nico and Anastasia. Before she reached the grand staircase she slipped through the doorway that led to the back stairs used by the servants.

The cool stone soothed her sore feet, but did nothing to help her aching heart. Nico didn't believe her. Nico thought she was lying. Nico thought she'd been with another man. She didn't know what else she could say to him. And in a horrible reminder of just how low she'd sunk every part of her was still throbbing from his heated possession. Once again he'd been hungry for sex, and once again she'd been willing. They were tinder and fire, verbally, physically… She might be strong in many areas of her life, but where Nico was concerned she could never find the strength to resist him.

The moment the sun hit her face Carrie looked for cover. If she was stopped now it would be hard to explain what she was doing in the palace—impossible if she wanted to avoid speculation and gossip. She could see a stone-roofed walkway that offered some protection, but if she took that route there was a point where she would be in full view of anyone standing on the balcony….

It was a risk she would have to take.

Hurrying along the passage, she fought the impulse to look up. But she had to, and then she saw Nico sipping champagne with the royal family.

It only emphasised his elevated status, and reminded her of the distance between them. And yet he stood apart from the rest, Carrie noticed.

She was deeply conscious of her bedraggled state and her bare feet as she reached the end of the walkway and stepped into the light, but she did so with her head held high. It was then Carrie noticed Princess Anastasia, and the princess noticed her. Walking up to Nico, Anastasia threw her arms around his neck and kissed him full on the mouth.

She couldn't bear to see Nico's reaction, but the pain of not knowing if she would ever see him again made her look up in time to see him wiping his mouth discreetly on the back of his hand. It was a small triumph, but inwardly she smiled.

Filled with renewed purpose, Carrie hurried to the gate.

She could feel Nico's gaze burning into her back every step of the way, but she didn't notice the shadow of an older woman watching her from an upstairs window.

CHAPTER SIX

SO MUCH had gone wrong that day Carrie couldn't wait to get back to the hotel, rest, relax and think about how to make it right. She had been sitting on a wall gazing out to sea for well over an hour mulling over the mess she'd made of things. She had given in to Nico, she'd had a row with him and she'd even managed to antagonise Princess Anastasia. What more could possibly go wrong?

Carrie knew the answer the moment she saw the smoke. Her hotel was on fire. Forgetting how sore her feet were, she began to run. Pushing through the small crowd, she captured the attention of an elderly man staring up at the firefighters. 'Is everyone safe?'

'Everyone's safe now,' he reassured her. 'The fire was confined to the kitchen, but it knocked out the electricity and so all the guests have been evacuated. They're just checking the upstairs rooms now as a precaution.'

'Thank you.' Carrie's first impulse had been to offer help, and now she knew there was no smoke or excessive heat to endanger her baby there was nothing to stop her.

'There's a lot of mess inside,' the man called after her. 'One of the firemen told me the kitchen won't be fit for use for some time…'

All the more reason for her to hurry, Carrie thought. She could only imagine how the owners of the hotel must feel. It would be hard enough trying to make a profit out of such a small concern without a disaster like this making things harder.

The first thing she saw was her small suitcase standing on its own in the hallway. Of course, all the other guests had gone, though there were plenty of people hurrying about trying to salvage what they could.

She followed the unpleasant stench of smothered fire to the rear of the building where she found more members of staff busily cleaning up, and there was an older woman on her hands and knees scrubbing the kitchen floor.

'Please, let me do that,' Carrie insisted. 'You've got enough to worry about.' Her heart went out to the older woman, whom she guessed had probably lost her livelihood that day. Her sleeves were rolled up, and her hands and arms were covered to the elbows in grime. 'If there's anything I can do for you…'

As the woman glanced up and smiled a weary smile Carrie knew kind words weren't enough, and with her permission she took the bucket of filthy water and emptied it in the yard. Swilling the bucket, she filled it with clean water and returned inside.

'Thank you,' the woman said, struggling to her feet.

'Please don't thank me. I'm happy to help…' Searching under the sink, Carrie found some detergent, but by the time she turned around the woman had gone. There was a lot to do, she reasoned.

Kneeling on a towel, she concentrated on finishing the job. The hotel fell silent as she worked, and the more she thought about it, the more certain Carrie became that the woman she had taken over from must own the hotel. She had worn the wounded expression of someone who had just seen her dream go up in smoke, which was probably why she felt a certain kinship with her, Carrie thought wryly, redoubling her efforts.

Straightening up at last, she clutched her back, knowing the effort had been worthwhile. The kitchen floor was sparkling again and it smelt fresh and clean.

'What on earth are you doing here?'

She nearly jumped out of her skin 'Nico?' Nico, angry? Nico, furious? But why? What was he doing here?

'I was assured that all the guests had been evacuated.'

'All, except one,' Carrie pointed out, refusing to be intimidated. 'What are you doing here, Nico?' she added, thinking him the last man on earth she had been expecting to walk into the hotel kitchen.

'You shouldn't be cleaning floors,' he said, shocked to see her...concerned for her safety, but he couldn't tell her that without putting ideas in her head.

'Thank you would be enough,' she assured him mildly. 'I don't know why you are so angry.'

'Did someone tell you to do that?'

'I'm quite capable of working on my own initiative.'

Carrie was surprised to see a tug at one corner of Nico's mouth. Had he found a sense of humour? Her rebellious body thrilled at the thought, though she stamped on it quickly.

'And how do you think you're going to get to the replacement hotel where all the other guests are staying?' he demanded, reminding her not to soften.

'I'll walk, or catch a taxi—'

'Don't be ridiculous.'

They both turned as the older woman who had been scrubbing the kitchen floor before Carrie's arrival walked back into the room.

'Mother!'

Mother? Carrie could only stare in amazement at the

older woman whom she knew now must be Princess Laura of Niroli.

'You'll do no such thing. Nico. You will take this young lady to the palace where she is going to be my guest... I insist,' she said, holding up one beautifully manicured hand. 'You knew you'd find me here,' Princess Laura observed fondly to Nico. 'This hotel was his father's wedding gift to me,' she explained to Carrie. 'To keep me out of mischief,' she added with a twinkle. And then, touching Nico's granite cheek with great tenderness, she whispered, 'Always so thoughtful, my Nico...'

As Carrie watched the brief exchange she wondered if Nico had a *doppelgänger*. His mother was certainly referring to a different man from the one she knew.

Swallowing back her amazement, she faced facts: the kindly woman standing in front of her was the grandmother of her baby. And Princess Laura had just asked her to stay at the palace. It was incredible. Unbelievable.

Conscious that she was staring rudely at Princess Laura, Carrie turned away, but not before her cheeks had reddened with suppressed emotion.

'We make a fine pair of cleaning ladies, don't you agree, Nico?' Princess Laura said.

'Without question, Your Royal Highness,' her son replied stiffly.

'No titles here, Nico,' Princess Laura insisted. 'And you can call me Laura,' she assured Carrie with the warmest of smiles.

'And I'm Carrie... Carrie Evans,' Carrie told her, starting to relax, though she guessed that his mother's approval didn't sit well with Nico.

'I think I saw you earlier, walking across the courtyard,' the princess observed. 'Don't look so worried—you weren't doing anything wrong. That's better,' she exclaimed, patting Carrie's cheek. 'I like to see you smile… Nico,' she added, 'please arrange for this young lady's luggage to be sent on to the palace. Carrie will be travelling with me, in my car….'

Carrie was still reeling from sweeping into the courtyard in an official limousine at the side of Her Royal Highness Princess Laura of Niroli, but she had never seen anything to compare with her suite of rooms at the palace. The main bedroom was like something from a fairy tale. White muslin billowed at the windows, and the vast four-poster bed was draped with ivory silk hangings. The cover on the bed was an exquisite testament of the quilt-maker's art. Intricately embroidered, it was delicately over-beaded in a ribbon design and the crisp white sheets and pillowcases peeping over the edge were finished with a froth of the finest lace.

Even the dressing table wore an elaborate skirt, Carrie noticed as the maid showed her round, and if the room wasn't quite to her taste it made her smile to think that such frivolity dared to raise its head in an increasingly uniform world. But this was the world of Niroli, Carrie reminded herself, where anything was possible, though it was hard to find a natural link between Nico and his mother, Princess Laura. The princess was so kind and warm, while Nico possessed none of his mother's ease of manner.

Nico…it always came back to Nico. Carrie's heart squeezed tight at the thought of seeing him again, something she could hardly avoid now she was staying at the palace. To try and calm herself she began to examine everything in the lovely room. Sunlight spilled through slatted blinds, and a fan whirred lazily overhead spreading the scent of lavender and rose water into the air. It was such a cosy room in spite of its size. It was a room where anyone could feel happy…unless they were looking forward to a confrontation some time later with Nico, of course.

The bathroom was another delight. There was pink Carrera marble on the walls, and a bath as big as a plunge pool. The ceiling was vaulted and lit with stained glass skylights, and there were enough luxury products on the shelves to start a small shop. The princess had insisted she must try everything, and had explained that luxury goods suppliers from all over the world showered the palace with gifts in the hope of gaining the prestigious royal warrant. Apparently Carrie would only be doing her a favour if she sampled them….

When Carrie awoke the following morning she wondered once again how someone as lovely as Princess Laura could have a son like Nico Fierezza. Carrie shook her head as she thought about it, but she would not allow Nico to undermine her confidence. Princess Laura had offered her the run of the palace and it would be churlish to stay in her room when the sun was shining and the gardens were so beautiful….

Surely. this was what the doctor had in mind? Carrie thought, closing the door on her apartment, when he had suggested that plenty of fresh air would be good for her baby…

He couldn't believe it. Carrie was staying in the palace at his mother's invitation! Which meant there wasn't a thing he could do about it; this wasn't his own home to order as he pleased. Having Carrie Evans out of sight was bad enough, but this, this was insupportable. As it was she played on his mind every minute of the day, distracting him when it was least convenient. Whether he liked it or not, a part of him always responded to her.

Loosening the collar of his shirt, Nico strolled across the room to the window. His apartment overlooked the lawns, and, beyond that, the lake. It was a pleasing vista...under normal circumstances. Grinding his jaw, he had to remind himself that his mother, in her infinite wisdom, had given Carrie the run of the palace. It appeared she was making full use of it now. She was running barefoot across the carefully groomed grass as if she didn't have a care in the world. Where did she think she was? The municipal park?

Turning away, he tossed his jacket on a chair and, peeling off his shirt, stalked into the bathroom. Carrie Evans was no concern of his. Loosening the waistband of his jeans, he let them drop and, shucking off his boxers, he switched on the shower and adjusted the temperature to ice-cold. Stepping beneath the freezing spray, he soaped down vigorously, then, rinsing off, he stretched to ease the tension in his shoulders. What he needed now was some strenuous exercise. What he needed now was space from Carrie Evans. But before that he had to confront her and find out what she was up to before this little game of hers got out of hand.

She had to be strong...With her head down Carrie ran across the endless stretch of newly mown grass and didn't stop until she reached the shade of some overhanging trees. She had just been talking to Princess Laura, and the princess had been so kind, which only made the deception harder to bear.

The fact that Nico's mother was the grandmother of her baby and she couldn't share the news was like a knife in her heart. Her child had been born into privilege, which carried with it huge responsibility, and a woman like Princess Laura would have been able to guide them both through the pitfalls.

Forgetting her baby's royal connections, any child would be lucky to have Princess Laura for a grandmother.

Sinking down on the mossy bank beneath the trees, Carrie curled up on the soft warm ground and made a silent pledge to her baby that she would make things right before she left Niroli. She stirred restlessly as the breeze ruffled the leafy canopy over her head, and then her eyes drifted shut.

'Have you any idea how this looks?'

Carrie jumped with alarm to see Nico standing over her. Shading her eyes, she tried to get her thoughts in order. The sun was low in the sky, so she must have been asleep for several hours….

'You can't just loll about on the ground here with your skirt round your neck.'

Carrie hurried to straighten her clothes. Nico made her feel so cheap. But she stood up too fast, and as she swayed he reached out to steady her. But the moment she was safe he withdrew his hand.

It told her a lot. It told her he didn't believe her. 'How long have I been asleep?'

'How do you expect me to know?' he said impatiently.

But he did know. He knew to the second how long she had been lying on the ground with her long hair spread around her. She was becoming an embarrassment. His mother had plied him with questions none of which he had chosen to answer. 'Did you plan this? Did you sit down before you came to Niroli and work out how to cause me maximum embarrassment?'

'Embarrassment? I fell asleep. Please don't think I'm taking advantage of your mother's kindness—'

'I don't think that. But you look so…untidy,' he said, for want of a better word to express his feelings.

'I don't have many clothes with me...' And then, tired of making excuses, she stood up. 'What is the appropriate outfit for walking in the palace gardens, by the way?'

His eyes narrowed as he studied her face. She had surprised him again with the softly spoken barb, and now his mind was awash with her fresh, sleepy scent. He had to forget how good they were together; he had to ignore the fact that there were leaves in her hair and he wanted to pluck them from the mass of tangled gold.

A greater contrast to the impeccably groomed Princess Anastasia would be impossible to imagine. Carrie's face was creased and blotchy where she had pressed it against the ground, and she looked...

'Can I go now?'

His gaze sharpened at her question. Her voice was as gentle as it always was, yet he sensed an edge behind it. She was anything but defeated. 'You've been very clever, worming your way into my mother's confidence. If one door shuts another opens as far as you're concerned, doesn't it, Carrie?'

'Do you think I started the fire at the hotel, too?'

'I'm merely suggesting you make the most of every situation.'

'What situation?'

'You didn't know it was my mother's hotel, of course.'

'Your mother's hotel? No, of course I didn't know. How could I?'

Her surprise appeared genuine. 'By reading about the family,' he suggested. 'You should know the Fierezzas have many interests on the island.'

'Which you imagine I researched before I got here? Do you really think I targeted your mother's hotel?'

'I think you're bright. I think you came to Niroli on a mission. And from what I know of you from when you worked for me I don't think you'd be here at all unless you had every loophole sewn up tight.'

'Well, that's where you're wrong, Nico,' she assured him. 'Where my personal life is concerned I don't seem to have much of a hold on it at all. And, for your information, it was the taxi driver who recommended your mother's hotel. He telephoned ahead as we were driving from the airport to book me in.'

'A quirk of fate?'

'If you like,' she said, 'but I certainly didn't engineer it.'

'And you want me to believe this, along with all your other lies?'

'I've never lied to you, Nico.'

The air between them was charged with tension. Nico was so close she could see the amber flecks in his searing blue gaze, so close they shared the same breath, the same air. But as always he reacted in a way that surprised her. Dipping his head, he brushed her cheek with his lips, stopping just short of her mouth, and to her eternal shame she closed her eyes and swayed towards him.

'It's that easy, isn't it?' he said gently. '*You're* that easy.'

When she didn't reply he put a finger beneath her chin and tilted her face up so she was forced to look at him. 'You wormed your way in here, and now you think you're going to have a good, long stay at the palace. Well, let me put you straight, Carrie Evans. You get twenty-four hours to live your dream, and then you're out of here.'

She closed her eyes against the contempt in his gaze. Nothing she could say would make him believe her, but she couldn't walk away. 'Whatever you think of me we have to talk, and I'm not leaving Niroli until we do.'

'Are you threatening me, Carrie?'

'I'm stating facts—'

'So, hell hath no fury?'

'You think this is about revenge?'

'What else?'

'You think I followed you to Niroli because I can't forget what happened between us?' That was part of the truth, Carrie realised, but she couldn't throw away her life on a hopeless cause, not with a baby to protect. 'You don't know me, Nico. You don't know me, at all.'

'Well, perhaps it's time I found out more,' he said coldly. 'Shall we start with how much it would cost me to get rid of you?'

Carrie flinched. 'Half an hour of your time is all I'm asking.'

'When?'

'Tomorrow night after dinner…' She didn't want to rush into anything, she had tried spontaneous and knew she wasn't good at it.

'I thought I made it clear that your deadline for leaving the palace is tomorrow…' Nico stopped and his face darkened with anger as he read the situation. 'Oh, I see,' he said. 'My mother has extended an invitation to her new protégée for dinner tomorrow night.'

'I'm sure you can spare me half an hour—'

'You're sure of a lot of things, aren't you, Carrie?'

'Until tomorrow, Nico…'

She turned on her heel, burning with shame from what he thought of her, but Nico brought her back. She held herself stiffly in his arms, eyes closed as she fought the urge to respond to him. But he knew she wanted to and with a sound of contempt he let her go and walked away.

CHAPTER SEVEN

'You poor child…' The words had burned themselves into Carrie's mind. She woke the next morning in her bedroom at the palace in a state of panic. Clutching the sheet to her chest, she gazed around, wondering where she was and who had spoken to her. Her mind was still sleep-drenched and wouldn't function properly. It took a few moments to accept she was alone and the presence talking to her was a voice in a dream.

Slipping out of bed, she padded barefoot across the room to open the heavy curtains on another soft Nirolian dawn. The view of the silver lake tinged with pink was so beautiful she stood for a moment with her eyes closed inhaling the scent of blossom. It could have been such a happy time if things had been different… If Nico had only cared for her, just a little.

It promised to be another hot day. The sun was already burning off the low-lying mist, and she could see the rowing boats bobbing lazily by the boathouse. It was easy to imagine Nico sitting across from her in one of the tiny vessels, his muscles flexing as he rowed her out on the lake… But as that was unlikely to happen she might as well have a shower, Carrie thought in her usual down-to-earth way; a long, cold shower.

She was becoming good at stretching the truth, Carrie

thought, rubbing her hair dry as she walked out of the bathroom, and it wasn't something she was proud of. To make matters worse Princess Laura appeared to accept everything she said without question. They had struck up a friendship based on a mutual love of the natural world and painting, but it was becoming harder all the time to hide her feelings for Princess Laura's son. There were no miracles waiting to happen, her dreams were futile, and her baby needed something more tangible than a daydream to secure its future.

Princess Laura had arranged for Carrie's breakfast to be sent up to her room. Seeing she was already dressed, the young maid insisted on laying everything out for her on the vine-hung balcony outside the small sitting room.

'Only if it's no trouble for you,' Carrie said.

'No trouble at all,' the maid assured her with a shy smile.

The princess, with her customary sensitivity, had found Carrie a cosy suite of rooms close to her own. Carrie's balcony overlooked a pretty walled garden with welcoming proportions more like those of the home of a friend, rather than the vast palace grounds.

'I prefer this wing,' the princess had told her, and then Carrie had discovered to her astonishment that they had adjoining apartments. 'Only special people stay here…' Princess Laura had said.

Carrie was living a lie she had no stomach for. She wanted nothing more than for the truth to be out in the open, but couldn't say anything while Nico stood like a roadblock in her way.

A discreet tap on the door of the apartment brought Carrie's pacing to a halt. But when she opened the door there was no one there… Then she spotted the envelope on the floor. Carrie's eyes widened as she read the handwritten note. It was from Princess Laura, offering her accommodation at the palace for the duration of her stay in Niroli, which the princess hoped would be for longer than a few days… 'We have far too many empty rooms here, Carrie, and I did enjoy your company. Please say you'll stay…'

As Carrie clutched the sheet of paper to her chest she knew that if she could have chosen anyone in the world to be the grandmother of her baby it would be Princess Laura, but Nico would never allow it. Princess Laura was everything a grandmother should be, but the princess was like a golden chalice hanging just outside her baby's reach.

This was one of the reasons he had left Niroli as a young man of seventeen, Nico reflected dryly as his mother advanced. Having finished his final lap, he checked his time: fifteen hundred metres freestyle in a few seconds over fifteen minutes. Not quite Olympic standard, but close. Planting his hands on the side of the swimming pool, he sprang out, water glistening over his tanned, athletic body.

Snatching up a towel, he buried his face to hide his smile. His mother was in full dragon mode. Behind a deceptively homely face Princess Laura hid a steely determination. He knew that was probably what had saved her when his father had been killed. Tossing his towel into a laundry basket, Nico was thankful for his mother's strength of character. She had been broken when she had received the news of his father's death, but had thrown herself into her charity work with renewed vigour, and that had been her salvation.

Straightening up, he wrapped a clean towel around his waist. Raking his hair into some semblance of order, he drew himself up to his full height…all the better to read the invisible banner his mother was waving above her head. It had a single name on it: Carrie Evans.

Carrie was going to stay *how long?* Grinding his jaw as his mother stalked back the way she had come, Nico vented his silent rage at the sky. He would not tolerate Carrie inveigling her way into the palace and winning over his mother into the bargain. The only reason he'd kept quiet was because he wasn't ready to reveal Carrie's state of health, or the lies she kept telling him. Fortunately, his mother didn't appear to know about the so-called pregnancy, but to be told by her to back off and stop treating Carrie like an underling was insupportable. And to be assured that she was under his mother's protection…

Right now he could cheerfully throw Carrie Evans over his shoulder and take her to the airport himself and put her on the first flight out of Niroli… But that wouldn't solve a thing, because, knowing Carrie as he did, she'd get the first flight back again. For now, he would tolerate her presence. He would wait his moment, and then he would expose her for the liar she was.

'You must have new clothes, my dear…'

Carrie had learned that Princess Laura didn't do questions, and that statements were more her line. She couldn't help smiling as she walked back towards the quaint arched doorway that marked the entrance to her apartment. When she had tried to tell Princess Laura that she didn't need any clothes the princess had silenced her with nothing more than an arched brow. There was a formal dinner that night, she had said, to which Carrie was invited. Carrie hadn't needed to be told that a market-stall dress wouldn't do for that.

And now the princess had worked her magic again…

Clapping her hands, she had invited dressmakers hovering just outside the open door to join them. And from that moment silks and satins, chiffons and jewelled net had been draped around Carrie, while pins and scissors had flashed in the light. A fabulous ball gown had been created where she stood.

It had been like a dream…

Maybe if it had been a dream she might have thrown herself with more enthusiasm into the pleasure everyone else was getting from her transformation, Carrie thought, but she knew that she would never belong to this life, and that Nico would never accept her. Hearing a tap on the door, she turned. 'Come in…'

It was the young maid again, who curtsied, making Carrie blush. 'There's no need for that,' Carrie assured her, and now the maid was blushing, too.

'These are your clothes, *signorina*.'

As Carrie reached forward to take a few garments from the girl she had to step back as footmen marched past her wheeling a collection of boxes and bags. 'There must be some mistake,' Carrie said with concern as she followed the footmen into her sitting room. 'I didn't order these…'

'But Princess Laura insists,' the maid told her.

Carrie guessed that when Princess Laura gave an order, no one, with the possible exception of Nico, dared to refuse her. And what could she do? The footmen were already unloading the trolley, and now the maid had disappeared into her dressing room and she could hear hangers clicking… drawers opening and closing again. 'Are you quite sure this isn't a mistake?' Carrie insisted, following the young girl into the room.

'Quite sure, *signorina*. The princess—'

'I know,' Carrie cut her off with a smile, 'the princess insists.'

As the young girl smiled agreement Carrie looked in awe

at her beautiful ball gown. It had been run up in record time, and looked even lovelier beneath the lights in her dressing room. Jewels twinkled on the bodice, and the note attached to it said... Carrie's heart sank as she read the words written in the princess's unique hand. She was to be Princess Laura's special guest at the top table, which meant she would be sitting with the royal family practically next to Nico. But how could she keep up the act that he meant nothing to her when he would be seated within touching distance and Princess Anastasia would be drooling over him?

She had to, Carrie told herself firmly, and she should be grateful to Nico's mother for giving her the opportunity to see Nico under such formal circumstances. If she acquitted herself well he might be inclined to spend more time with her after the meal.

She had nothing to feel embarrassed about, Carrie told herself, glancing at the dress again. Princess Laura had wanted her to feel comfortable at the banquet, and had ensured that the dress she wore was beautiful. The dinner was going to be a glittering affair and it was unlikely anyone would have packed something suitable for an occasion such as this one in their holiday suitcase. She could borrow the dress for one night, and then hand it back. She could have it cleaned first... she would ask the young maid, or the girl at the boutique, where to go. This wasn't the time to be trying to find an excuse not to go to the banquet; this was the time to seize an opportunity.

Reading through Princess Laura's note again, Carrie knew she couldn't refuse. 'Please do come, Carrie,' the princess had written. 'I must have someone decent at my side. These events can drag on so without the right company....'

Decent? The word tolled like an accusation in Carrie's

head. She was about as far from decent as… It made her wish she could tell the princess everything. Their conversations had spanned so much, but had never ventured towards the baby. They had even talked about Carrie's ambition to become a professional artist one day, when she had almost forgotten how much she wanted that, herself.

She looked up as the maid politely excused herself, saying she would be back later to help Carrie dress. Carrie thought a walk through the grounds might help to relax her in the meantime. She had an idea forming, and was eager to look at the gardens with an artist's eye. Her intention was to paint something special for Princess Laura to thank her for her kindness.

Carrie found several spots where she would have liked to set up her easel. There were winding paths and woodland glades as well as the more formal gardens. And then, of course, there was the lake and the pavilion… The grounds of the palace went on and on, and she was glad she had brought a pad and pencil so she could make a start with some preliminary sketches.

Slipping off her sandals, she ran across the cool, spiky grass towards the lake. But she drew to a halt long before she reached the water's edge. Nico was there with Anastasia, and the princess looked so beautiful. She was wearing a slim sheath in brightly coloured patterned silk that hugged her slender body like a second skin, and high-heeled shoes, which Nico was making her take off before allowing her to step into the rowing boat. And now Anastasia was laughing and holding on to his arm as she slipped off the first shoe. When both shoes had been removed Anastasia secured a large-brimmed straw hat to her head and then looked up expectantly at Nico…

Nico didn't respond, he was gazing away across the lake,

Carrie noticed, and seemed distracted, and then very slowly he turned towards her…

He stared at her. Nico stared straight at her. It was as if they had an invisible bond between them. But then the princess, unused to losing anyone's attention for even a moment, took hold of his sleeve and gave it a little shake. Nico turned back to her, and with a gracious smile and a nod he offered Anastasia a steadying hand as she prepared to board the small boat.

They made a perfect pair, Carrie thought. They were both so good-looking, so confident. They made her feel shabby and insignificant by comparison. For a moment, she wanted nothing more than to run back to the palace, but her feet seemed rooted to the spot, forcing her to watch Nico as he climbed into the small craft. He stood with his legs planted firmly to steady it, as Anastasia settled herself in front of him. Anastasia laughed as he cast off, and the sound carried across the silver water like a well-bred reminder of Carrie's place in life.

Hardly knowing she was doing it, Carrie narrowed her eyes to study the perspective. There was nothing more romantic than watching a man putting his back into a stroke. She gave a little smile as Nico pulled away from the small jetty, and was on the point of returning to the palace when she heard Anastasia calling to her. She certainly had no intention of slinking away. Turning, she smiled and raised her hand to wave.

'Oh, look, darling…it's that little girl from your office. Doesn't she look quaint in that sweet little dress? Good morning, dear…'

As the princess trilled her greeting Carrie's jaw firmed. An air rifle and a few well-placed shots below the waterline of the little boat might not have gone amiss… Failing that, a reef, though no doubt Nico would negotiate it safely.

But as the boat pulled away and they both lost interest in

her Carrie felt stupid and gauche, and the market-stall dress that had been such a life saver in the heat seemed suddenly dull in comparison to Anastasia's glamorous designer outfit. Then Nico turned as if to check that she had gone, and the look he gave her suggested he knew how she felt about his beautiful companion.

He could think what he liked; she was going to stand and take in every detail… It was more fuel for her paintings.

As Nico increased his stroke the chalky pink scarf the princess wore around her neck floated out behind her. It finished the picture and made Carrie long to paint the scene…the swarthy hero with his shirtsleeves rolled up to the elbow, exposing his powerful forearms, the wide spread of Nico's shoulders and the flex of his muscles as he drove his oar through the water. The tension in his legs beneath his jeans…

In fact, Carrie thought mischievously, she would be quite happy to leave Anastasia out of it. It would make a much better painting, she concluded, turning away.

CHAPTER EIGHT

As SHE prepared for dinner that night Carrie was excited and apprehensive in equal measure. She was also doubly determined not to let Princess Laura down. She fully intended to look her best. But when the maid went to collect her dress they discovered that a calamity had occurred.

The first Carrie knew of it was a distraught cry that brought her running into the dressing room. 'Are you all right?' she said anxiously, drawing the girl into her arms when she saw how upset she was.

'Your dress…the beautiful gown… I can't find it.'

'But it can't have disappeared,' Carrie said sensibly. 'Come on, let's look for it together. We'll soon find it. You start at one end of the rail and I'll start at the other…'

But as they searched Carrie's confidence began to falter. She flicked determinedly through the press of garments a second time. There were so many gowns to search through. If there was one thing she had learned it was that Princess Laura didn't do anything by halves. Once the dressmakers had taken her measurements they must have been sewing non-stop. But there was only one special gown for tonight, and it was nowhere to be found.

She hid her feelings from the maid, but she had lost more than a gown, she had lost her chance to make Nico see her differently....

'Maybe you could wear another dress, *signorina?*' the maid suggested in desperation.

Carrie's concerns switched immediately to the young girl's disappointment. 'What a good idea. Let's look for one together,' she suggested, forcing a bright note into her voice.

But there was nothing to compare with the matchless gown, and after a fruitless hunt the maid suggested checking all the other dressing rooms in the palace in case there had been a mix up of some sort.

'Whatever's happened to the gown it's not worth crying about,' Carrie assured her. 'And it's too late to start searching the palace,' she pointed out logically. With the maid on the verge of tears again she had to be practical, but it wasn't easy when the loss of the dress was such a bitter blow.

'Please, let me go and look for it, *signorina,*' the maid pleaded with her. 'You never know, I might find it.'

'All right, but I don't want you to worry if you don't. This isn't your fault. While you're gone, I'll have another look through the wardrobe. I'm sure I'll find something else to wear.'

Carrie picked out several formal dresses and then discarded them again for various reasons. Some of the necklines plunged to the waist, which with her voluptuous figure was hardly prudent, and others had slits almost to the crotch. All the shoes seemed to have spindly heels, and she dreaded wearing them, but time was marching on and there was still no sign of the maid returning.

Carrie glanced out of the window and her throat dried as she caught sight of the stream of limousines rolling in procession along the road towards the palace. Their passengers would be ambassadors and billionaires, and enough European royalty to fill the pages of a celebrity magazine. Princess Laura had wanted to prepare her for this, and had wanted her to feel comfortable in such elevated company, and now everything had gone wrong. She glanced at the door, she couldn't wait for the maid any longer. She wouldn't risk being late for Princess Laura. She would just have to choose something else to wear....

But now Carrie made another worrying discovery— everything in the wardrobe was at least one size too small. It didn't make sense. Princess Laura's dressmakers had been so thorough and precise with their measurements and she found it hard to believe they would have made such an elementary mistake. She began to suspect someone had done this on purpose to humiliate her.

Returning to the wardrobe, she selected a beaded sheath with an impressive fishtail train, for no better reason than it fell off the hanger at her feet and she took it for a sign. Now she just had to hope the Fates were on her side.

Having shoehorned her way into the dress, Carrie found she couldn't fasten all the tiny silk-covered buttons that ran up the back. Glancing at the clock, she grew increasingly anxious. For her to walk into the banqueting hall after the king had sat down was an unimaginable breach of etiquette, and she had no intention of embarrassing Princess Laura.

So where was the maid? Had she been hijacked along the way? Carrie was beginning to think that the loss of the gown was no mistake, and that perhaps the maid had been sent on some new, time-consuming errand by the same person who had removed the gown. Because the dress had been taken, Carrie thought grimly as she battled with the buttons.

The only way she could secure the dress she had chosen

was by tugging it round, fastening the buttons, and then heaving it back again. Unfortunately by this time her cheeks were beetroot red, and her carefully dressed hair was hanging in tangles. Gazing at herself in the mirror, she felt like crying. The jewelled bodice barely covered her big bouncing breasts that threatened to erupt out of the confines of her gown at any moment. She looked a mess, and now it was too late to choose something else to wear. The fabulous couture gown didn't hang on her as it was supposed to. It clung in a most unflattering way, revealing every cream cake she had ever consumed in her life. And she still had to choose some shoes….

How could she choose when she couldn't bend over? Hopping around, she managed to hook some stratospheric stilettos with her big toe. 'Lengthen your line' —wasn't that the advice for small, plump people in women's magazines? She had certainly done that, and had become a five foot nine walking disaster along the way. Grabbing a handful of hairpins as she tottered towards the door, she stuck them in her mouth, intending to stab them into her hair as she hurried to the banquet.

Carrie made a conscious effort to slow down when she reached the main reception room and tried to copy everyone else, but that wasn't easy when she was so uncomfortable in the ill-fitting dress and could hardly walk a step without falling off the wobbly shoes. As if that weren't bad enough, everyone but her was part of a couple, or a group….

She would just have to play a role. She was tall and elegant…she was a woman of the world, confident and self-possessed. She was utterly at home in the palace….

Well, she was until she reached the double doors and saw Princess Laura waiting for her. The princess was talking animatedly with a group of friends, and looked stunning in full-length lilac chiffon. Her gown was sprinkled with diamanté and she wore a glittering tiara on her head. She had dainty beaded dancing slippers on her feet…and, though Carrie tried hard not to look, Nico was standing at his mother's side.

She was furious with herself for allowing Nico to affect her so badly. Gazing around, she searched for an escape route. All she needed was a few minutes alone to compose herself and then she'd be all right….

A few minutes in the fresh air would be perfect, Carrie decided, spotting a door into the garden.

The footmen in attendance quickly opened it for her, and the moment it clicked shut behind her she breathed a sigh of relief. Just as she'd thought, it was better, cooler in the garden. She took several deep, steadying breaths and only a couple of minutes went by before she felt ready to return.

But as she turned Carrie noticed that the lights in the corridor had been switched off. Going up to the door, she pressed her face against the glass. The footmen were nowhere to be seen. Trying the handle, she found it locked.

She wasted precious minutes in a panic, rattling the handle, and staring down the deserted corridor, until she finally accepted that she would have to find another way in.

The light was fading rapidly and the towering walls seemed so dark and oppressive. And she couldn't even be sure she was heading in the right direction… The substitute gown with its heavy beading was like a suit of armour, and agitation had sent her internal heating system into meltdown.

Hearing voices, she sped up. The palace kitchen, Carrie realised with relief. The doors had been left open to allow the heat to escape….

There was a lot of good-natured comment as she made her way gingerly through the banks of cookers. She didn't dare to touch anything, and the walkway was slippery beneath her feet. Her face was growing redder by the minute, and she knew without touching it that her hair was standing off her head in a frizz. There was a serving area at the end of the room and a queue of waiters standing ready. It was too late now to worry about committing the cardinal sin of appearing in the banqueting hall after King Giorgio. She had no other way of getting in, and, having accepted Princess Laura's invitation, nothing was going to stop her.

Nearly overbalancing, she staggered back into her shoes, and then, making her excuses, she squeezed through the waiting staff. The man standing guard at the door was so taken aback by the sight of her that he forgot to stop her walking past him.

The first thing she knew was light so strong it blinded her. The glare from a dozen chandeliers blazed straight into her eyes, along with the flash of diamonds, the glint of silver and the sparkle of champagne… Expensive scent hung in the air along with the cooler smell of privilege. There was no heat around her now, just a stunned and icy silence as rows and rows of faces turned her way.

Hearing a nervous laugh, Carrie realised she was the only person in the vast room who found her situation remotely amusing. And there must have been five hundred people or more in the banqueting hall, including the royal family seated on a raised dais. And now the waiters were pressing at her back, and she had no way to turn around….

And then, incredibly, Nico was at her side. Her chest was in a vise at the sight of him and she could hardly breathe. Nico helping her to straighten her dress… Nico steadying her as she tried to take her first wobbly step…

'Wait,' he snapped.

She clung gratefully to his arm, keenly aware of the solid strength of him. Being with Nico validated her presence at the banquet. And, of course, he was immune to the titters and murmurs coming her way…unkind comments that were very quickly dying away.

And now there was only silence. But still Nico appeared in no hurry to move forward. He stood as if everyone was lucky to have this opportunity to feast their eyes on them. And as far as Nico was concerned she had to admit that he was right. He was dressed splendidly and wore his official uniform with pride. On any other man it might have appeared effete, but on Nico it only emphasised his blistering masculinity.

But she didn't need him to put her on a leading rein. She could manage perfectly well without him. 'Nico, I'm quite capable of—'

'Not now, Carrie.'

Taking her hand, Nico locked her in his grip, giving her no alternative but to accompany him. Halting at the foot of the dais, he bowed to the king and indicated that she should do the same. 'When is this going to end, Carrie?' he murmured as they lowered their heads, and then, raising her up again, he led her forward to join the royal family.

By the time she was seated next to Princess Laura, Carrie felt as if someone had drawn a running thread through her stomach and pulled it tight. And there was no softness in the princess's gaze, just a look that willed her to be strong. She had only been in her seat a few moments when Nico leaned down to murmur to his mother, 'Don't worry, Mother, I'm sure I'll be able to find another chair.'

Realising her mistake, Carrie blushed and went to stand up again, but Princess Laura stopped her.

'He's quite old enough to look after himself,' she said with a twinkle.

Glancing up, Carrie thought she saw a flicker of amusement on Nico's face, too. Was he laughing at her?

As he sat down Nico reflected that he had just shared the warmest look with his mother he could remember for years. It seemed Carrie's pluck had impressed both of them; she had certainly taken the stuffiness out of the occasion. How long since he'd relaxed like this at a state banquet? How long since someone had broken all the rules only to endear herself to the king? Who couldn't take his eyes off her, he noticed now. Driven to move closer to Carrie, he moved his seat to sit next to her.

Carrie tensed as Nico came to sit beside her. She was aware of nothing now but his mocking gaze on her face.

'My mother tells me there's been some mix-up over your gown,' he said, leaning closer. 'I'm sure there must have been. Do something about that, will you?'

He was staring straight down her cleavage.

'And what do you suggest?' Carrie demanded, though she could feel her face turning red when she checked. Her breasts had almost escaped the confines of the uncomfortable bodice and she had to make some speedy adjustments in order to avoid a very public disaster.

'Charming,' Nico murmured, bringing his face even closer. 'Such style and grace… As a royal guest you make a very good sideshow, Carrie Evans.'

'If you had listened to me in the first place, I wouldn't be here,' Carrie pointed out tensely.

'But then I would have missed this…'

'Perhaps you think this is funny, because you're used to events like this, and can relax. But I can assure you that being laughed at by everyone isn't remotely funny for me—'

'Carrie, no…' He tried to stop her as she left the table, but she was too quick for him. She even managed to fit in a curtsy to the king and to his mother before picking up her skirts and fleeing the dais.

And now she left him no alternative but to go after her.

He caught up with her outside where she had stopped to slip off her shoes. 'What on earth do you think you're doing, running off like that?'

She ignored him and started tugging up the awful dress around her thighs. 'Stop that!' he insisted, glancing round to see if anyone else could see.

'I have to walk somehow,' she said, sniffing loudly.

She was crying, he realised, but her legs were the most shapely legs he'd ever seen and he didn't feel like sharing the sight of them with any of the other guests. 'If you take my arm you won't need to do that,' he offered gruffly.

Take his arm? To wrap it round his throat, perhaps! 'Thank you…' Carrie could see the sense in Nico's suggestion, even if she didn't like to admit it. She was having enough trouble coping with the dress when she was walking on a level surface, let alone trying to keep her balance on the steps. Loath though she was to accept Nico's assistance, she knew she couldn't risk a fall.

But once she took his arm Carrie realised she had made a tactical error, because all she was aware of now was Nico's warmth and his strength and the intoxicating tang of his cologne.

'Where would you like me to take you, Carrie?' he murmured, no doubt expecting her to say, straight to bed.

'To my room, if you please…' She was quite proud of herself. She sounded like a heroine in a period novel. But anything less and the game was over.

'Very well,' Nico said, playing along.

Her mind was full of the touch of his mouth and the warm possession of his tongue, she could feel his hands moulding her limbs, directing her pleasure, increasing and prolonging it… And then as he plundered her mouth she would open for him like a flower, and—

Here they were. What a relief. 'Thank you,' she said politely, disentangling her arm from his at the door. 'I'm going to see the evening through,' she informed him. 'I gave my promise to your mother, and I won't let her down. I'm going to shower now and see if I can find something more suitable to wear. I'd like you to apologise to the king for me and to your mother, of course, and say that if they will allow me to I should like to join them for coffee.'

'And do you expect me to escort you back to the banqueting hall, too?' His voice was mocking, but he admired her spirit, even if he knew he shouldn't fall for it.

'Thank you. That's very kind of you,' she told him politely.

He turned his back without giving her chance to respond. His feelings were colliding: mistrust with admiration. She had suffered terribly from the frosty reception she had received in the banqueting hall and most people would have had enough. He could have told her that the royal family had appreciated the interlude, and that he had, too, but did she need any more encouragement? He doubted it. She was determined to face them all again. He had to admit he would have done the same thing, and could only applaud her decision to return.

Carrie couldn't have been more thrilled for the young maid. Not only had she managed to track down the elusive gown, she had uncovered the culprits. The gown had been discovered in Princess Anastasia's dressing room.

'I can't think how it got there,' the maid said, shaking her head in disbelief.

'An honest mistake, I'm sure…' Carrie didn't want any more trouble, she wanted an end to the matter. She had far more important things on her mind, and the first of these was winning Nico's trust. A catfight with Princess Anastasia would do nothing to further her cause. If she acted with dignity now it gave her a platform from which to go forward.

After a quick shower, with her hair pinned up, Carrie stepped into the dream gown. Slithering the cool silk over her warm, naked skin was a wonderful sensation. The dress had been cut to display her smooth, pale shoulders to best advantage, and hint at the full swell of her breasts without putting them crudely on display. The maid had found her a pair of soft kidskin mules in the same delicate shade, which she slipped on smiling with relief, because they felt like slippers. Daintily beaded, they had a low heel that made it easy to walk gracefully, and as a finishing touch the maid handed her a gossamer shawl.

'In case the evening turns chilly,' she said, adding a neat evening bag with a silk strap that Carrie could hang from her wrist.

Having made sure everything was as it should be, the young girl invited Carrie to sit in front of the dressing table so she could arrange her hair. She pinned it loosely in an artful knot, allowing some tendrils to fall free and frame Carrie's face. Then, plucking two fragrant blooms from a display of blush-pink roses, she secured them in place.

Carrie stared at her reflection in disbelief. 'I can't believe it. I feel beautiful….'

'You sound surprised, *signorina,*' the young girl said happily, 'but you are beautiful.'

Carrie was sure the maid was only being kind, but kindness went a long way with her. 'I appreciate the trouble you've taken on my behalf,' she said sincerely, levelling her gaze on the young girl's face.

'I am Princess Laura's personal maid, *signorina*, and the princess asked me most particularly to look after you.'

As the young girl hurried away Carrie couldn't help feel more optimistic than she had since arriving in Niroli, but then she remembered Nico, and his suggestion to escort her back to the dinner. She wasn't sure she was ready for that. And why should she wait for him? Why give him the impression that she was incapable of acting independently of him? It was essential to behave as she meant to go on if she was to win the best chance of a happy future for her baby.

But the thought of facing that gathering a second time had drained the colour from her face. Opening the powder rouge she had bought on a whim at the airport, she brushed a little onto the apple of each cheek. She wasn't going to let a few butterflies stop her. Next she applied some lip-gloss and mascara, and lastly, a fluff of powder, and now she couldn't think of a single reason for delay.

He glanced at his watch again. He'd had no contact from Carrie.

He couldn't wait any longer. She would be in a panic if he kept her waiting. He had no intention of risking another and possibly far more eventful scene in the banqueting hall.

He had half risen, and was about to murmur something to his mother, when he caught sight of movement by the grand doors. Pausing, he refocused and then sank down again slowly in his seat.

Carrie had just entered the room unescorted. With some satisfaction he noted that just as he had taught her she paused by the door. Her appearance stunned everyone. Perhaps he gasped like the rest, he wasn't sure. She looked…exquisite. Her bearing was regal, her manner gracious…and she was beautiful, truly beautiful. He couldn't believe the transformation; he couldn't tear his gaze away from her. When he did, it was to see the footmen bowing as if she were the most exquisite creature they had ever seen, they were enchanted by Carrie.

He tried to analyse the changes in her in order to understand them. Her pale skin was flawless, and her blue eyes backlit with warmth and intelligence. But it was more than that, she was radiant, and had instantly won the heart of every man in the room. She had acquired dignity in the space of an hour, and perhaps even more appealing than that was the glow of her indomitable spirit, which shone brighter than any light.

He had become as still as everyone else, Nico realised. It was as if the whole room was holding a collective breath, waiting to see what she would do next. He didn't even want to go to her in case he broke the spell, he just wanted to sit where he was and feast his eyes on her, but then her steady gaze met his…

They held the heady stare as Carrie slowly began to walk forwards, until she stood just in front of Nico. 'You look beautiful…' It wasn't enough, not nearly enough, but he couldn't find the words. He only knew that the woman standing in front of him was complex and elusive, and he wanted her.

'Thank you.'

It seemed incredible now that it was Carrie who was self-possessed and he who was struggling for composure. He was so proud of her. He would never have guessed she possessed such confidence, or such elegance. The simplicity of the couture dress suited her. The designer had wisely concluded there was no need to flaunt her assets, knowing that to the connoisseur they were more than apparent beneath the cunningly cut silk. He found himself standing back to give her space, to show her respect, and then he found himself bowing low from the waist to her as he might to a queen.

CHAPTER NINE

THE speeches seemed endless, and with Nico seated next to her Carrie found it hard to concentrate. It had become like musical chairs at the royal table, with Anastasia having persuaded someone to move so she could sit next to Nico. He was a charming and practised dinner companion, and appeared content to share his time between Anastasia and herself.

Princess Laura did her best to distract Carrie with amusing anecdotes from Nico's childhood, which Carrie guessed not many had been invited to share. She had to admit they made him seem almost human, but then she reminded herself that this was his mother talking, and Princess Laura clearly adored her children. Anastasia's laughter proved a constant distraction, reminding her that whatever compliments Nico had heaped on her initially she could never compete with an international beauty like the princess. As if to rub it in, Nico glanced at her from time to time, perhaps to check that she was behaving properly and not disgracing him.

It was after a particularly lengthy clash of stares that Carrie sat back with her heart thundering. She should have known better than to try and boldly stare him down. There had been an edge to his expression she had recognised at once. It hadn't been the look of an employer, or a prince; it had been the look of a man who wanted a woman in his bed.

That was how Nico would always see her, Carrie reflected, staring down at her hands. However he'd behaved towards her when she'd walked into the hall she remained a convenience upon whom he expended his excess energy. Princess Anastasia, on the other hand, was playing for far higher stakes.

'You seem preoccupied…'

Carrie started with alarm. She hadn't even realised it was her turn to receive Nico's attention. As always the quick-witted remark escaped her, and he had already turned back to Anastasia who had found some reason to distract him by the time she had composed herself.

The next speaker received Carrie's full attention. The elderly king made a point of welcoming Princess Anastasia to Niroli, and then went on to extol her many virtues. Nico murmured agreement, Carrie noticed, feeling her confidence slowly leaching away. King Giorgio went on to hint that one day his grandson Nico might find himself on the throne. This came as a huge and unwelcome surprise to Carrie. She had never imagined Nico aspired to the throne. A king would have no place in his life for a child born out of wedlock, and a woman careless enough to become pregnant by him could only bring shame on the house of Niroli. Nico hated gossip, and he had always avoided the possibility of becoming tainted by it. How much more determined would he be to do that if he were King?

She didn't even know she was wringing her hands until Nico's warm touch stopped her. Before she had chance to consider what he'd done and why, the waiters, who must have received a signal to refill their glasses, came between them.

Did Nico care about her feelings? Had he changed towards

her? Did he believe her now? Carrie so wanted to believe it was true that when the orchestra struck up and Nico rose to his feet she half rose with him. But instead of turning to her he offered his arm to Anastasia.

She felt humiliated as she watched them bow to the king, and then Nico escorted Anastasia onto the dance floor. It was the first dance, Carrie told herself firmly, determined not to let her feelings show. Princess Anastasia was the guest of honour, and Nico was expected to dance with her; it was his duty….

But nothing helped to soothe the hurt inside her and every minute seemed like an hour as the dance went on and on… Anastasia was so proud and regal in Nico's arms, appearing to everyone, Carrie was sure, as if that were her rightful place… How could she stand it?

The answer came straight away. For the sake of her child she could stand anything.

'Well done,' Princess Laura whispered so discreetly Carrie couldn't be sure she had spoken at all.

He returned to the table after executing his duty with as much good grace as he could muster. Carrie had gone very pale, he noticed, and would barely look at him. His grandfather seemed pale and unwell, too.

In the short time he had been in Niroli he had noticed his grandfather's deterioration and could understand his urgent wish to find an heir. He could step in and put an end to the old man's suffering right away. Accepting the crown was the only thing his grandfather had ever asked of him, and King Giorgio's increasing weakness brought out the protective elements in his nature. He could think of endless reasons why he shouldn't accept the crown, but now he tried to find reasons why he must. He would see more of

his family, and maybe in time he could bring his head office to Niroli and learn to live happily within the confines
of a small island….

Work and rule? Nico frowned as he flicked the edge of his
jacket out of reach of Princess Anastasia's spiny fingers. He
had always been an all-or-nothing man. Ruling Niroli would
mean relinquishing his business completely. But as the princess
reached for him again a smile curved his lips… If he were King
he could have Anastasia banned from the kingdom for ever.

Easing himself away from her, he wondered how much
more he was expected to take of Anastasia's suffocating per-
fume and desperate manner. And now he was forced to jerk
his leg away as her bare foot tried to find his calf. The woman
revolted him. He had done his duty by her as custom
demanded, but the thought of bedding her….

Swallowing back disgust, Nico turned his mind to solving
the problem of an heir should he take the throne. He had no
doubt he would make a good king. He was an effective leader,
and so far there hadn't been a problem he couldn't solve.
And, he reminded himself, he had two brothers who could
provide an heir….

But as Anastasia released a theatrical sigh he glanced at
Carrie. She still had her face turned away from him, showing her strong profile, but there was something vulnerable
beneath the surface that touched him. The contrast between
the two women couldn't have been more marked. He decided
to test his thoughts on his mother. Leaning across, he drew
her attention. 'I could settle at court pretty quickly with
Anastasia at my side, don't you think, Mother? She seems to
have every bit of etiquette at her fingertips…'

His mother appeared not to hear him.

'As a princess born and bred,' he pressed mischievously,

'don't you think Anastasia would slip easily into her role as my wife?'

'Your wife?' His mother turned abruptly. 'Why, Nico,' she exclaimed, bringing her face very close so they couldn't be overheard, 'I thought you could tell a real jewel from a fake, but it seems I was mistaken.'

He sat back, feeling more pleased by that comment than he had expected. Thrusting his jacket aside, he stuck his thumbs into the pockets of his waistcoat to continue his contemplation of Carrie. She so quiet, so modest and discreet... It pleased him to think that only he knew the other side of her. And now he ached to be alone with her. He ached to be inside her.

He felt a rush of pleasure when she turned to look at him. She had sensed his interest. Meeting her gaze, he indicated with the faintest quirk of his brow his intention to leave the banquet. She hesitated, and then, just as he had expected, she quietly stood and curtsied low to his grandfather. The king was too busy talking to notice her, and his mother was back on the gossip trail. Below them on the dance floor couples swirled in a kaleidoscopic whirl of colour. Any remaining guests were chatting easily at their tables now the wheels of conversation had been oiled with good food and wine. No one would miss them if they left, and he didn't care if they did; some things wouldn't wait.

Pushing up from his seat, he inclined his head politely as Carrie drew alongside him, and then, offering her his arm, he escorted her from the room.

'Nico?' Carrie said faintly, when Nico, having opened the door to her apartment, showed no sign of leaving.

'Aren't you going to ask me in?' he said.

Ask him in and face the consequences? Ask him in and fulfil her role as his convenient woman? She couldn't even call herself his mistress, Carrie reflected. She was nothing more than Nico's bedmate, the woman who eased his frustration when he was bored or restless, or had a few minutes to spare before his next engagement. 'Won't Anastasia miss you?'

His lips tugged up at that, while his eyes burned with some inner heat. He had no intention of answering her, she knew that, but she still wanted him with all her heart, her soul and every inch of her body. She wanted to lay claim to him, to put her brand on him, to push Anastasia out of the picture once and for all.

She saw the humour growing in his eyes as if he knew every thought passing through her head. And his humour was so much more potent than lust, because it suggested the intimacy between them she craved. That was why it always managed to slip beneath her guard….

And was she supposed to resist the confident curve of Nico's lips, or pretend she couldn't hear the beating of her own heart? Heat was rushing through her before he even touched her. She was blind to reason the moment she felt him looking at her and wanting her. The thought of instilling common sense into their relationship no longer mattered to her. All she wanted was to feel Nico's arms around her and his lips claiming her mouth. She was his, she would always be his, and she couldn't, she wouldn't fight it….

Taking him by the hand, she drew him inside the room and closed the door. She could feel the tension draining out of him right away. This healing process, this coming together and finding release, was as crucial to him as it was to her; it was as vital to their existence as air. When he ran his fingertips down her naked arms she didn't sigh, she vocalised a sound of love, of need and urgent hunger. And Nico understood that.

Of course he understood. They spoke the same language when it came to this….

'Kiss me,' Carrie murmured, throwing back her head to expose the tender hollow at the base of her neck. She was already vibrating with anticipation. She was ready for Nico in every way. And when he kissed her, when his tongue plundered her mouth, it was all she could do to remain on her feet. Desperate for further contact, she pressed herself up against him, moulding her body to his, and rejoicing in the surge of passion between them, exulting in the strength of his embrace. The insistent pressure of his erection between her thighs wasn't enough. She wanted to possess him, and for him to possess her. She wanted him, on any terms…

On any terms?

'No!' Turning her head away, she made the exclamation softly on a sigh, and then she pushed him away, directing what little will she had left into the movement. 'You can't have everything you want at your command, Nico.'

Carrie heard the words and couldn't believe that she had spoken them.

Nico didn't reply, and in the space when she should have been more tongue-tied than she had ever been it was she who found the words: 'I can't do this anymore, Nico. Not anymore…' It is destroying me. She didn't say that, she only thought it, and somehow she held herself together when he turned and walked away.

She had a cruel dream that night. In her dream Nico stayed with her and they had made love. They had made love as she had always wanted to, with tenderness and with emotion. Staring deep into her eyes, Nico had told her that he loved her, and she had believed him….

But then, of course, this new Carrie had been a princess who wore a beautiful gown and lived in a palace. This new Carrie had had the confidence of knowing she was adored, and that Nico was only one in a long line of adoring suitors. This new Carrie hadn't made it so shamefully obvious that she loved Nico Fierezza to the extent she wasn't aware any other man existed. And this new Carrie had been subtle and clever and quick-witted and beautiful, and had lured Nico deep into the room merely by crooking her finger at him and smiling her ravishing smile.

Equally matched, they had made it to the bed, which had made them laugh. This time it hadn't been on a table, or up against the wall, or anywhere Nico found convenient, but a bed…a big, comfy bed where lovers who trusted each other could spend more than a few fiery minutes in each other's arms. They could spend the night together and share their secrets. And then they had started laughing as they had rolled together, tight in each other's embrace, and then they had begun to fall, and fall… And then she had woken up to find it was only a dream; a dream that had left her emptier than she had ever felt in her life.

Clutching her knees, Carrie buried her face and faced the truth. Far from loving her, Nico had left her last night the moment he had realised she wasn't his to use and discard as he pleased. She almost wished she could turn the clock back and behave differently. But if she did that she would only be walking the same lonely road leading nowhere. She had exerted her will, and she had proved that she could do it, and now she must continue down that same, equally lonely road. But better to be strong than weak, for what kind of role model would she be to her child if she were weak?

Perhaps if she could leave Niroli and all the hurt behind… But she knew now that her dream of hiding away in the countryside was a foolish fantasy that took no account of a cruel world where a child of privilege was a potential target. She couldn't take the risk that the truth about her baby might leak out; she couldn't do anything that might endanger her child. And now she had a ten o'clock meeting with Princess Laura. It had been arranged between them before everything had gone so badly wrong. 'A girl's induction to palace life,' the princess had described it, knowing nothing of the undercurrents and deception behind Carrie's presence at the palace. Having insisted she stay on, Princess Laura had said it wouldn't hurt Carrie to be prepared. For anything, Princess Laura had added with her customary twinkle.

Maintaining the deception with Nico's mother was fast becoming an unbearable agony. And one she had brought on herself, Carrie reflected, straightening up. She would keep her promise and meet Nico's mother as arranged. How could she not when she still had to thank Princess Laura for the loan of the beautiful gown?

Everything had changed in the space of a few hours, forcing him to examine his feelings for a woman whom he knew to be a liar, and yet who last night had worn the mantle of integrity like a shining cloak. No one could infuriate him more than Carrie; no one could soothe him as she could, either. But she had withdrawn her comforting hand, her calming presence, and had chosen to drive him away. His lips curved briefly with appreciation, remembering her show of spirit at the very moment when he had been so certain she was his. It had made him want her like never before and perhaps had enabled him to see her clearly for the first time. He had certainly seen enough to make some significant changes to his thinking. Carrie's quietness masked her determination and her indomitable will. In that he had underestimated her hugely. She might look like a delicate wildflower in comparison to the woman his grandfather had chosen for him, since Anastasia reminded him of a garish silk bloom in an undertaker's window, but Carrie was strong. If she hadn't lied to him he would have wanted more than sex from her, but how could he pursue a relationship based on deception? The fact that she was pregnant by another man was tearing him up inside, but even that wasn't enough for him to want her out of his life.

Princess Laura's tour had been so interesting and informative, and the princess herself so kind and generous with her time. Carrie felt guiltier than ever. She wanted nothing more than to tell Princess Laura the truth about her baby, but she couldn't say a word until Nico accepted his child.

Princess Anastasia's name had come up several times during the day, and Carrie had been surprised to hear Princess Laura say that she found Anastasia tiresome. It had made Carrie wonder what kind of stepmother Anastasia might make if she and Nico did decide to marry.

By forcing Nico to acknowledge his child would she be condemning her baby to the very life she so desperately wanted to protect it from? A life where her child would always fall short in Anastasia's eyes? Not to be loved was the greatest pain imaginable, and it was the last thing she wanted for the baby growing inside her.

Carrie's agitation grew to the point where she considered leaving Niroli without saying another word to Nico. She could leave a discreet note of thanks propped against the dainty clock on Princess Laura's dressing table... She could call a cab to take her to the airport, and then disappear somewhere so impenetrable that no one would ever find them...

It took a huge effort of will to banish the doubt as she had banished the weakness, but she did so by reminding herself that at some point she had to believe in Nico. She had to believe he was the man she thought he was, the man who would always protect the weak, and who would protect his children with his life.

She fixed a smile to her face as the young maid hurried back to her side with some fresh flowers that she had picked herself to pin to Carrie's dress for that evening. The young girl still believed in happily ever after and it wasn't fair to stamp on her dreams. 'Once again you've made the perfect choice for me,' Carrie assured her. She could live the dream for one more night, couldn't she?

The simple gown was ankle-length in honey-coloured silk. It had long sleeves and was demure, yet the cut showed off her figure to best advantage. When she was dressed the maid insisted she must secure her long hair behind a simple headband and then leave it loose.

'But I look so young,' Carrie complained. And she wasn't sure that that was such a good thing where Nico was concerned. Having taken a giant step forward in standing up to him, she didn't want him mistaking her this evening for someone who would be grateful for his guidance. But then she caught sight of the maid's expression in the mirror and knew she had disappointed her. The fact that she was wearing her hair loose wouldn't make her any less determined.

The maid smiled with relief when she agreed to the hairstyle. 'I hope you enjoy your evening, *signorina*,' she said, having added the finishing touches.

Somehow Carrie doubted it, but she found a confident smile. 'I'm sure I will,' she said with resolve.

CHAPTER TEN

THE MEAL HAD dragged on for far too long. Nico's gaze lingered on Carrie's face. It shone with vitality, and with honesty, and with all the qualities that constantly challenged his opinion of her.

Sensing his interest, she turned to look at him, but almost immediately turned away again. Her chin was firm and her mouth set in a determined line. She was gaining in confidence every hour under his mother's expert tutelage, to the point where tonight she might have been the princess and Anastasia the impostor. The king was clearly enchanted by her, his mother, too, and only he remained to be convinced. And yet it pleased him to see how well she conducted herself under the most shameless barrage of patronising remarks he'd ever heard from Anastasia. The woman had no class at all. The only reason he hadn't stepped in to defend Carrie was because she had given him one of her looks, warning him to keep out of it. After that, he had to admit he had rather enjoyed watching her parry and thrust as if she had been schooled for years in repartee. She had behaved with all the dignity and restraint of a woman to be admired, a woman who knew her own mind and would defend her own corner to the last... *A woman who would defend her children with everything she had...*

With a frown of impatience he looked away. Whether or not Carrie made a good mother was no concern of his.

But one thing was certain: this wasn't for him. He shifted restlessly in his gilded chair. He'd sat down long enough. The stifling restrictions at court took his mind back to his reasons for leaving Niroli in the first place. But he had no intention of leaving the island until he had settled all outstanding issues. Only then could he give the king his final answer.

Standing up, he bowed first to his grandfather and then to his mother. 'Carrie… I believe you wanted to speak to me?'

The silence at the table was complete as Carrie, having curtsied prettily, came round the table to him. He felt a surge of triumph at her quick compliance after her rebellion the previous night, but he masked it as he murmured politely to his mother, wisely avoiding her perceptive gaze.

'I'm glad you took the hint,' he said to Carrie, easing his shoulders as the footmen closed the doors behind them. 'I couldn't have stood another minute of that woman's company.'

He had to be referring to Anastasia, Carrie realised, but was that a sop to her feelings, Nico's way of opening negotiations and encouraging her to lower her guard? She had no intention of lowering it, but outright conflict wasn't the way to win with Nico, so she would seize the opportunity he'd given her to talk to him in private.

As Nico matched his stride to her much shorter one Carrie thought he had never looked more handsome, or more desirable. She could feel the tension between them that had always led to passion in the past. And now she noticed a scar at one corner of his mouth. Why had she never noticed that before? What else had she missed? The scar only added to the impression of a hard man trapped in a world of cloying ceremony. But for how much longer? Did Nico seriously intend to accept the throne?

'We'll go straight to my apartment,' he said, heading in that direction.

He had taken it for granted she would follow him. Her words last night might never have been spoken. He found it inconceivable that she could hold out against him, and believed everything was back to normal now. Why shouldn't he think that? She had left the banquet promptly at his signal, and now she could read his intentions perfectly: Nico was impatient; Nico wanted exercise, and not just to stretch his limbs or his intellect; Nico wanted sex. She was on hand, she was available, and time was wasting...

'Well?' he said, stopping mid-stride. 'What's wrong? Why are you holding back?'

'I thought perhaps the library...' She glanced away from him across the hall.

'The library?' He frowned.

'I'd like a coffee... Or tea, if you'd prefer.' She held his gaze steadily, hardly daring to breathe.

'I thought you wanted to talk to me in private?'

It was a code between them. His hard mouth had softened in a way that she knew so well. 'While everyone's at dinner, the library should be empty, don't you think?' She watched a muscle work in his jaw, and knew she'd made him angry. For one nerve-wrenching moment she was sure he was going to turn on his heel and walk away from her, but then he inclined his head abruptly in a gesture that invited her to lead the way.

Her heart was pounding as she walked into the library. Resisting Nico never got any easier, but she had to stay strong or each time she weakened he would tighten his control over her, and she wanted more for her baby than a mother who provided extra services for her boss. She loved Nico with all her heart, but, however much it hurt her to admit it, it was the love of good sex that fuelled his interest in her. Plus Nico was attracted to anything different from the norm, and she was the surprise beneath the plain brown paper wrapping, the mouse no one suspected of being a tigress in his bed. She was the perfect mistress, in fact, the woman who was interested in no other man.

She would never stop loving him, Carrie accepted as the library doors closed behind them, because she loved Nico for what he could be, and not for what he was.

Their order for coffee was taken immediately. That was how Nico's life was run, Carrie reflected. His every whim was accommodated, even anticipated, and as far as he was concerned she was just another member of his staff to provide services as and when required.

While they waited he stood with his back to her, showing his disapproval of her change in manner from eagerly compliant to unpredictable. She remained perched on the edge of a leather chesterfield and didn't move until the maid returned with a tray. At that point Nico turned to say he didn't wish for them to be disturbed, and that he would ring for the tray to be removed when he was ready.

Carrie didn't wait to be asked, she poured coffee, and then offered one to Nico, which he refused.

'I think we both know we're not here for coffee.' He was prepared to be reasonable, if only to inhale the special scent she wore. He liked it. It soothed him. It was light and delicate like the wildflower he often thought her…the wildflower that could turn into a thistle, he reminded himself impatiently.

He gave her more than enough time to say what she had to say, and he made sure to listen intently to every word. He even maintained his impassive expression when she repeated the lie, uttering the words he had been longing to hear all his adult life. She was pregnant, and, she wanted him to believe, by him.

He closed his heart to her, comforted by the knowledge that the test he was about to take would prove her a liar. Knowing it to be pointless, he had never taken a fertility test before, but he had booked one now. As a member of the ruling family he was assured absolute discretion and priority treatment.

What was wrong with Nico? Carrie wondered as his stare hardened even more. His manner had encouraged her to choose this moment to speak to him, but now she felt she had misjudged it. It was almost as if he knew something she didn't, and that it was something to her disadvantage. "The truth that makes men free is for the most part the truth which men prefer not to hear…" The quotation sang in her head, prompting her to say again, 'Whatever you choose to believe, I am pregnant, and you are the father of my child.'

The doctors had been quite specific when they had told him he had been lucky to survive the childhood illness that had struck him down as a youth. The fact that he would never have children was a small price to pay for his life, they had assured him. He expected nothing from the fertility test, but as Carrie held his gaze a kernel of uncertainty crept into his thinking. To even accept the possibility he could father a child would require one of two things: a sizeable change of mind-set, or a scientific test. He'd go with science.

The knowledge that he couldn't father children had for ever been a deep-seated grief that had always prompted Nico to risk more, to fly higher, race harder, jump farther. And when his father had been killed he had seen how life could end in a moment, which had been all he had needed to keep on challenging fate in the belief that he had nothing to lose.

Until now…

If there was the smallest chance Carrie was carrying his

child she must stay with him. Medical reversals were not unknown, and this was one risk he was not prepared to take.

'I'll leave you to think it over,' she said, reclaiming his attention.

He bridled as she opened the door. Was the conversation over? He didn't recall drawing it to a conclusion. She was defying him again, perhaps to see how far she could go, but she had picked the wrong man to try these tactics on. 'Sleep well,' he said, knowing she would toss and turn without the comfort they always brought each other.

He fully expected her to turn, to stop at the door, to relent and run back into his arms as she always did.

'You, too, Nico...' Opening it quietly, she slipped through it like a mouse.

He didn't read the report they handed him in the hospital. Instead, he tucked it inside the pocket of his trousers, and didn't look at it again until he was miles out of town.

He had a stallion to prepare for the annual Palio race, and the horse had been only too pleased to allow him to work off his frustration. Reining in at last, he dismounted and slipped the reins over its head, allowing it to graze on the thin brown grass, which was the only nourishment to be found on the lower slopes of the mountain.

'You'll drink later, when you've cooled down,' he promised as the stallion whinnied and nudged his arm.

The horse had scented the icy water that ran in torrents from the peaks, but he couldn't allow it to drink yet, not while it was still sweating. Bringing his face close to the velvet muzzle, he shared a breath with the beast he was sure would win the Palio. 'Not yet, Fuoco, I'll tell you when it's safe to drink, just as I'll keep you safe in the race.'

The horse was well named—fiery both by name and by nature. He would win…if they stayed alive. The race through the old town was full of risk. It took less than two minutes, but involved fierce and dangerous competition. The cobbles were unforgiving to a horse's hooves. 'We'll keep each other safe, Fuoco,' he murmured, and then with a confident laugh he slapped the horse's neck and moved away.

Taking the envelope out of his pocket, he found a suitably dramatic vantage point to read the single sheet of paper. Lodging his foot on a rock at the edge of a cliff, he gazed out, knowing he could drown in the glories of nature if all else failed. Right now he felt as if there were a firework display going off in his head…a firework display full of colour and possibility; the possibility of a child….

He prepared himself for disappointment. Before reading a word he balled his hand into a fist and watched the knuckles turning white. Concentration helped him to steady his breathing. He hadn't hesitated over anything in his life before, but this was different.

He could have a child. The knowledge overwhelmed him in waves, and with them came a sense of urgency such as he had never experienced before. If he was the father of Carrie's child, he wanted to be with her immediately. If her child was his then it was his to love and to protect, and there was no question of her giving him ultimatums, he would decide what they did from here.

He could hardly contain his relief when he saw her, and it took a supreme effort of will for him to hold back on what he had to say to her until lunchtime. There was no question of failure and so he had made certain preparations first. He had sent a message with one of the footmen, inviting her to eat with him on the terrace overlooking the lake. He had left nothing to chance. He wanted to surprise her, but above everything, he would control the situation.

'I'm glad you decided to join me,' he said when she arrived on the terrace. She had made a particular effort with her appearance, which he took as a good sign. The soft colours suited her, and the casual clothes were perfect for what he had in mind. 'Shall we take a stroll, first?' he suggested. 'Or would you like to eat right away?'

'I'd like to talk, Nico.' Her gaze was steady and her voice was annoyingly firm.

'But there's something I'd like you to see…' He rose from his seat. He wasn't prepared to accept defiance.

Her answer was to dip her head in a way that might have meant yes, or no.

'I think you're going to be surprised,' he said, waiting impatiently for her to fall into line.

'Pleasantly, I hope?' she said, and there was a touch of humour on her mouth.

'I hope you think so…' He heard the bite of irritation creep into his voice, and had to work to suppress it. 'Shall we?' He offered her his arm. She declined and chose to walk alongside him…not close enough.

He took her on a leisurely tour of the palace, wondering where on earth he found the patience to do so. He was consumed by the knowledge that he could be a father. He wanted to take her into a room, shut the door, tell her the truth, and demand she follow him into the world of testing and certainty. But that was no way to gain her trust, and if he wanted a good relationship with the woman who might be carrying his child, he had to show more subtlety.

They viewed many of the private treasures that weren't

available for public scrutiny, and by the time they reached the
narrow staircase leading to the turret he had relaxed a little.
She had shown such interest in everything, asking him
probing questions about how his ancestors came by such
riches, which had made him smile in spite of everything. But
now they had reached the only part of the tour that really
mattered to him. He was certain that when she saw what he
had prepared for her she would forget her newfound determination to defy him and come back to him with all the softness
of his mouse, and all the love in her eyes he had been accus-
tomed to seeing before hard-edged had become a bad habit.

It was the most romantic setting Carrie could have imagined…a tiny turret room at the very top of a tower where the
light was perfect. She knew it was perfect before she even
asked Nico the question. 'North-facing?'

'The perfect aspect for an artist's studio,' he confirmed,
watching her closely.

Carrie's excitement abruptly died. Nico must have done his
research well to be so sure of her response. Like everything
else he had made it his business to find out about her before
bringing her here. He had never cared enough to do that
before. Carrie's suspicions were coloured with sadness as she
looked around. It was so easy to think she could switch off her
feelings for Nico, but she never could. If only this could have
been one of those happy moments without strings attached,
the type of moment she had never known with him.

But now? Everything in his manner warned her there was
more to this than met the eye. When was Nico ever so strung
out, unless he was waiting for sex? Though she sensed something very different was driving him now.

'Please disregard the mess left behind by a previous tenant…'

He was trying to make a joke of it, but even he couldn't force humour into this situation. Noticing the jumble of unused articles stacked against the wall for the first time, Carrie realised that she had only seen the potential for an artist's studio when she had walked in. Nico was right about the room being perfect for that. The views stretched for miles around, and space and light like this were everything she had ever dreamed of. But he knew it, and was using it as a lever.

A lever for what? To make her his official mistress, perhaps? Madam Carrie Pompadour of Niroli? Carrie tried to smile, but, like Nico, she was a million miles away.

As Nico stood watching her Carrie knew he was waiting for her to say something. What could she say? He was everything she had ever wanted; she didn't need anything else. Her honest response to this clumsy gift was a heavy, leaden feeling in her heart. It wasn't enough, and if it had been it had come far too late.

'What do you think?' he prompted.

'I'm not sure what I'm supposed to think. What are you offering, Nico? A studio I can visit from time to time?' Carrie shook her head sadly. 'What?'

Nico's eyes narrowed with affront, shattering her heart in a million little pieces. He wasn't used to his gifts being rejected, and he'd had little time to organise this 'gift,' making it all the more valuable in his eyes. Perhaps if there had been more time he would have found an easel, palette and paints... a larger bribe. But a bribe for what? To accomplish what? For her to be in his bed when he wanted her? Had he even registered what she had told him about the baby?

'I've ordered oil paints for you...'

The fact that he had read her so well only filled Carrie with more dread. Nico was always one step ahead of her. When she returned home she had planned to rent a small place, and had envisioned a north-facing room just like this one where she would paint in great swathes of colour... She was determined that her child would inhabit a brightly coloured world, not a dull grey world without the chance of a dream coming true.

She couldn't afford to waste another moment of her time on pointless quests, Carrie realised. Hugging her stomach protectively, she took one last look around.

Her simple gesture caught him by surprise. Always, she thought first of the child, and only then herself. He found himself overwhelmed by emotion, so many of them, and all of them new to him... He felt wonder and tenderness and excitement, along with a deeply primitive urge to share the remaining months of Carrie's pregnancy with her and then to raise their child and have the baby live beneath his protection. She couldn't take that from him, he wouldn't let her. 'This is for you,' he stressed impatiently when she didn't turn to him right away. 'I did it for you,' he said again, waiting for her to enthuse. 'I just want you to be happy.'

'Happy...'

'You're going to be a mother soon.'

Carrie's heart soared. So he had accepted that, at least.

'And it is my child?' His brows furrowed.

'You must know it is...' Her confidence faltered as she looked at him. 'Nico, there's something you aren't telling me, isn't there?'

'Maybe,' he admitted.

'So what is it?' She felt fear in the silence that stretched before he spoke.

'After an illness I suffered as a boy the doctors told me I would always be infertile.'

Carrie's eyes widened in amazement. It was Nico's turn to be speaking too loud and too fast, but she now understood so much about him. 'And now?' she said gently.

'Now I know I'm not.'

'How?' she asked, her compassion for him blinding her to the obvious.

'A test.'

He was holding on to her gaze like a life raft, and then he grew guarded again, as if he expected her to find fault with him now.

But that was so far from her thinking it didn't even register on the scale. Recognising his Achilles heel, she reached out to him. 'Oh, Nico…' Taking his work-roughened hands in hers, Carrie brought them to her face and laid her cheek against them.

CHAPTER ELEVEN

THE MOMENT Carrie softened towards him Nico rejoiced. 'You could be carrying my baby…' As he said the words he barely knew how to contain his joy. The test had changed his whole outlook on the world…on Carrie, on him, on everything.

'Could be?' Her voice was still gentle, still low, but anxiety had broken through.

'And if you are,' he went on, brushing aside her concerns, 'you'll stay with me—'

'Is that an invitation,' she said more firmly, 'or are you forbidding me from leaving you, Nico?'

He was surprised by the change in her, especially after she had shown him so much tenderness. He should have expected it. And after the way she had behaved last night he should have been prepared for it. He wished he could pinpoint the moment Carrie had changed and wind back the spool to a time when she had been more accommodating. But whatever she said, there was no scope for compromise; agreement with his plan was the only course open to her.

'I thought… I hoped,' she amended, 'that when I finally convinced you about our baby you would rejoice as I have done—'

'And I am rejoicing,' he assured her.

She remained unconvinced, and turned away from him to stare out of the window.

She wasn't seeing the view. She couldn't see anything from the turret except the dust and grime of neglect. The studio was an afterthought; she was an afterthought, and the only thing Nico cared about was becoming a father.

'Obviously, I can't know for sure if I'm the father of your child until the baby is born,' he said, breaking the silence with harsh fact.

'And then?' She turned back to face him.

'And then a simple test can be performed. The whole procedure is quick and painless…a swab inside the cheek… samples delivered for analysis…results available quickly… By return, in fact, because—'

'Because you're a member of the royal family?' she supplied, staring out of the window again.

'Don't make this any harder than it has to be, Carrie—'

'Harder?' She looked at him, puzzled.

'You don't seem to realise what I'm offering you.'

'You want me to take a test. I think I got that part.'

As she looked at him he saw a variety of emotions colour her gaze. There was affront and distress, but then she settled on the one he expected least, and didn't want, and that was pity. 'I thought this was what you wanted…' He gestured around the room.

It was as far from what she wanted as it was possible to get. But whatever Nico said, however deeply he cut into the love she felt for him, she would never find a way to excise him from her heart. That was a fact she had to live with. And perhaps he was right, perhaps she was being unreasonable. Wasn't this why she had come to Niroli? Nico was on the point of accepting their child, so shouldn't she forget about how she felt about their relationship and think about the baby?

'You wouldn't have to stay in Niroli if the test proved negative,' he went on, as if she had already agreed.

If the test proved negative? Was he serious? Did he think there was the remotest chance she would lie to him now? It saddened her to think how little Nico knew her. She knew him. She knew he had felt his infertility like a missing limb, and that he had wanted a child so badly it had coloured his whole life, making him court danger like a man with nothing to lose. His harsh manner was aimed at warding off anyone who might come too close to him, anyone who might discover his secret, the secret of his infertility. 'You must decide what you want to do——' He cut her off before she could say the rest.

'I'm glad you understand,' he said as if he were closing a deal. 'And when the baby's born there'll be another simple test——'

Carrie held up her hand to silence him. Everything in her rebelled against the thought of some unnecessary procedure being carried out on a newborn infant.

'It's a simple, non-invasive test,' Nico went on, reading her thoughts. 'It involves blood being taken from the baby's umbilical cord——'

She wasn't hearing him. She wouldn't listen.

She rounded on him then, her face contorted with passion. 'You don't get it, do you, Nico? It's *my* baby...mine and yours! And I won't allow our baby to be subjected to a barrage of tests just to prove something I already know!'

The strength of her reaction shocked him. She was shouting at him in a way he would never have dreamed she was capable of, and when he took a step towards her she waved her arms in his face to drive him away.

'Don't touch me, Nico! I've heard enough! I thought you wanted to talk to me because you were keen to work out the best way forward for our baby, but instead you insult me and our child with your talk of tests. You don't believe me!' she shouted when he tried to take hold of her. 'You don't believe me!' she repeated bitterly, wrenching herself free.

'Calm down, Carrie! This can't be good for the baby—'

She went instantly still, so still she frightened him. 'Don't you dare express concern for my child, when you're not fit to be a father!'

He'd heard pregnancy drove emotion to fever pitch in women, but he'd never realised what it could be like. He waited as she hugged herself for her shoulders to relax before trying again. 'I'm trying to make this easy for you, Carrie—'

'Easy?' she said incredulously, swinging round.

'I have accepted the fact that you are pregnant,' he said patiently, 'I have also accepted the fact that you might be carrying my baby—'

'Might?' she interrupted. 'Might be carrying your baby? You have accepted that? Why, that's very good of you, Nico—'

'I want you to be happy, Carrie—' He was forced to stop as her eyes filled with tears. After her anger it was like a pendulum swinging too violently, first one way and then the other. And as she gazed around the room in the turret where he'd made his clumsy attempt to keep her in Niroli guilt hit him like a sledgehammer. 'Please listen to what I have to say.'

'No, Nico.' She shook her head, calmer now. 'You've got nothing to say that I want to hear.'

When she went to move past he dragged her close, but she remained stiff and unresponsive.

'Let me go, Nico. We're finished here.'

He couldn't let her go. 'Not until you agree to my terms.'

'Your terms?' She looked at him sadly.

He let her go. He released her arms and stood back. He had never used his strength against a woman in his life. 'I'm offering you a home, Carrie—'

'Like a stray dog?'

'Like the woman who might be carrying my child. You don't have a home in London, and you have very little money—'

'Your investigations do you credit, Nico.'

'Did you expect me to sit back and do nothing?'

She shook her head, too miserable to say a word.

'I've made plans.' He wanted to see her smile again and knew she would see the sense in them. 'We'll announce our engagement right away, and then be married shortly after that.'

Nico was proposing marriage to her? Carrie's mind reeled. And then she realised he was waiting for her answer.

'It makes sense, Carrie,' he insisted.

'You say marriage makes sense?' She was vaguely aware that he was nodding his head, encouraging her on. 'And what comes next, Nico?' She looked at him. 'A speedy divorce? Or, better still, an annulment? And what happens if the tests prove you are not the father of my child?'

'Is that a possibility?'

'If the tests are carried out in Niroli I should think anything is possible for a member of the royal family.'

He reared back at her accusation. 'Please don't insult me, or my country.'

'Don't you insult me with your shoddy suggestion of a meaningless engagement and a loveless marriage!'

'Perhaps I should reassure you that Niroli has a state-of-the-art hospital where everything will be carried out without the donors even being named. There will be no interference with the samples, I give you my word. And I would never agree to a procedure that might inflict discomfort on a baby.'

'On *our* baby,' she corrected him.

It was time for her to face facts. Nothing had changed as far as Nico was concerned. A side of him she had always believed existed had made a fleeting appearance, but she had always been in danger of believing what she wanted to believe where Nico was concerned. He had asked her to become his wife, which was a dream come true, except that dream was now a nightmare. His offer was nothing more than a tactic to hold her in place until their baby was born and Nico could find out if he was the father. 'You don't have to marry me,' she assured him. 'All I want is that you acknowledge our child—'

'If the child is mine you can have anything you want.'

If if if! 'I've told you I don't want anything!'

'So you don't want royal protection for your baby?'

All the old fears returned. Everything paled in the face of her baby's safety, and her budget would never stretch to the type of security Nico was talking about.

'Any child of the royal family would receive protection as a matter of course,' he went on smoothly.

Whatever she did for her child would never be enough. She needed professional help with protection and that cost more money than she had. 'Can't a formal agreement be drawn up between us to allow for security measures to be put in place?'

'A formal agreement? Marriage is a formal agreement, and under the terms of that agreement any child of ours will be entitled to protection under the legislation of Niroli.'

Carrie felt the blood drain from her face. Nico had thought of everything and spoke so glibly about marriage. He made it sound like any other business contract with nothing more than legalese to bind them together. She already thought of herself and the baby as one entity, one family, while Nico was still looking at the future from the viewpoint of an individual. 'I don't want to marry you, Nico.'

'What?' His expression turned black. 'Why not?'

'Because you don't love me.'

'What has love got to do with this? I thought you wanted security for your child.'

The mockery of a loveless marriage…was that what Nico thought she wanted? Surely, everyone wanted and deserved to be loved? 'So, we'd enter into a marriage of convenience to tie everything up neatly?'

'Exactly,' he said with relief.

'But I don't want that.'

He was growing impatient. This should have been straight-forward. He was offering Carrie a brilliant match. A family was everything he had ever wanted, and as far as he could see this was the perfect contract with benefits on both sides. The tests were essential; he had no intention of taking any unnecessary chances. A marriage was easily dissolved, but he could not acknowledge a child until he was certain.

'This is how it's going to be,' he said, feeling sure Carrie must be reassured by the thought he had put into his plan. 'You will agree to marry me in order that your child is protected. I'll take care of your baby, Carrie, whatever the out come of the test.' From her expression he couldn't be sure that she had grasped the significance of his offer. 'Whether the child is mine or not,' he stressed, 'you will both have my protection.'

'And if I don't agree?' she said quietly.

He couldn't believe she was still prevaricating. 'You agree, or you have nothing,' he said bluntly.

'And this offer of marriage is not because you love me, but

because you won't take the chance of a royal baby being born out of wedlock?'

Her analysis of the situation was bitingly correct. 'It's your decision.' He eased off, confident now of the outcome. No woman would walk away from the wealth and status he was offering her.

The very last thing he expected was for Carrie's face to darken with anger.

'You still think this is about money, don't you, Nico?' Before he had chance to answer that, she added, 'Money means nothing to me, and as for your royal status…' A look was enough.

'Brave words, Carrie, but haven't you forgotten something?'

'My child? My baby is always at the forefront of my mind, Nico. By refusing your offer of marriage I'm protecting my baby from a man who doesn't know how to love. Don't you think I know that the only reason you've asked me to marry you is because you can't be certain whether or not I'm carrying your heir?'

'I'm not prepared to enter into a discussion,' he said flatly, 'Those are my terms. You can take them, or leave them.'

'Then, I'll leave them,' she told him with contempt. 'And please don't trouble yourself with my transport arrangements. I can find my way to the airport without your help, too.'

It wasn't that easy. He couldn't let her go. The woman who might be the mother of his child. Unthinkable! He'd give her a chance to calm down and then he'd go to her and make her see reason. 'Take your time to think about what I said,' he called after her as she left the room.

He couldn't be sure she heard him, and stood motionless until he could no longer hear the report of her angry feet on the stone steps. He took one last look around at the offer she'd rejected and then he followed her down.

It irritated him to know she was right about many things. How had he ever thought her a mouse? She had more character than he knew. He mustn't rush this. He'd take a stroll around the grounds to give her time to come to her senses. Staying with him was a big decision, but she'd come round to it.

He loved having Carrie around, Nico reflected as he strolled across the lawn. Being with her was a real roller-coaster ride but even now he found himself looking for her in her favourite spot by the lake. He felt alive when he was with her, and even his days as an adrenalin junkie seemed numbered with Carrie who was enough adrenalin for anyone.

And she was having his baby.

The rush that hit him was the best he'd ever known. He didn't need the test to be sure. She was the only woman he had ever wanted; she was the only mother he wanted for his child. The mother of his child would be brave and have spirit like Carrie. He would do anything it took to make her see his point of view, and if that meant renouncing the throne of Niroli, then he'd do that, too.

CHAPTER TWELVE

SEALING the envelope, Carrie got up from her dainty seat at the delicately carved escritoire by the window in her sitting room to ring the bell. When the footman arrived she handed the letter to him. 'Would you be kind enough to deliver this to Princess Laura for me, please?'

'Certainly, *Signorina* Evans.' With a dip of his head the footman went swiftly about his duty.

As Carrie took a last look around she knew she would never forget these few days in Niroli, or the kindness she had been shown. She was sad to be leaving, and knew how lucky she was to have been invited to stay in a palace, and luckier still to have made a friend like Princess Laura.

The note she had written to Nico's mother was the coward's way out, but she couldn't risk the princess trying to persuade her to stay. After a bout of morning sickness Princess Laura had guessed she was pregnant, though as yet, she didn't know who the father was. She had to leave Niroli before Princess Laura discovered the truth. Things had reached such a pitch with Nico she had no alternative. She had to go before Princess Laura found out and decided to take up her case with him, or, worse still, concluded she was nothing but a conniving trickster who had wormed her way into her affections for the sole purpose of engaging the support of a powerful ally.

She wouldn't risk losing the friendship of a woman she had come to admire, Carrie thought as she locked the catches on her suitcase. The best way forward for her was to seek legal advice in England. She had wasted enough time on some schoolgirl notion that Nico was entitled to know about his baby. Nico had forfeited his right with his suggestion of a marriage of convenience. She had to go home and get on with her life. All that remained was to wait for the taxi to take her to the airport and her time in Niroli would be over.

'Under what circumstances did Ms Evans leave the palace?' Nico was seething with rage as he towered over the royal attendant. 'Why wasn't I informed of her departure immediately?' He bit down on the rest of the questions thundering in his brain. He had always believed hectoring servants to be the mark of a bully. And if the man had known, it was more than his job was worth to pass on below-stairs gossip. 'Never mind,' he said crisply.

Closing the door, he leaned against it and exhaled heavily. Having failed to contact Carrie by telephone, he had visited her apartment only to find it empty. He had searched the grounds and the palace, and even the old town, finally bringing himself to confront his mother who had refused to see him and had sent her manservant to tell him that thanks to him Carrie had flown home to London.

Flown home to London? London was a big place, and, as far as he knew, she didn't have a home to go to.

Crossing the room, he picked up the phone. It wasn't in his nature to chase after something, or someone in this case, without proper preparation. In this instance the only preparation he needed to make was one call to Airport Security to have Carrie stopped at the departure gate.

It should have been simple, but he was stopped by a phone call from the king's office. His grandfather wanted to see him at once. 'The king will have to wait.' He ignored the gasp of astonishment on the other end of the line, though he softened his refusal with a brief apology. And then his mother rang, begging him not to throw away his one chance of happiness.

What chance of happiness? He stamped down hard on the accelerator pedal of his sleek grey Aston Martin. Only he knew what it took to make him happy, and so far everyone in Niroli had gotten it spectacularly wrong. It wasn't the throne of Niroli, or an advantageous marriage to Anastasia. It was Carrie, Carrie Evans, his mouse.

Before leaving the palace he had written a formal letter renouncing all claim to the throne of Niroli. He had claimed exemption through one of the ancient rules: 'No member of the royal house may be joined in marriage without previous consent and approval of the ruler. Any marriage concluded against this rule implies exclusion from the house, deprivation of honour and privileges'. He was going to marry Carrie for love, not convenience, and she meant more to him than some arcane hokum. Carrie had shown him an alternative way to live his life. His answer had been to throw the opportunity she had given him back in her face. And now he had to catch the London flight before it left or risk losing her for good.

He was too late. He couldn't have put his feelings into words if he had tried. Gazing at the empty sky, he couldn't even find a vapour trail to track her journey back to London. He had no idea where she was heading, and she hadn't left a forwarding address.

Because she had none, Nico reminded himself, already

concerned about Carrie's welfare. Turning from the wall of windows, he vented his frustration with a vicious curse.

She had been staying in a modest guest-house until she found a suitable apartment to rent. It had taken her less than a week. She knew the small mansion flat was the right one for her the moment she walked outside onto the glazed balcony.

'I'll take it,' she said without hesitation, oblivious to the chaos left by the previous tenant. With the small bequest from her parents she could afford the three months' deposit—as well as a bag of cleaning products.

And this wasn't a tainted dream like the studio in the turret; this was happy reality, which she had made happen. Not that it was enough to keep the sadness at bay. But as she stared at her paint-smudged reflection in the mirror she knew she should be thankful that she could pay for every inch of space and every pot of paint herself. She had done with office suits and crisp white blouses. She had done with standing in line waiting for Nico to notice her, or to come up with any more cold-blooded schemes. She had her life back, and very soon there would be another life to consider. But it still hurt when she thought about Nico Fierezza, and perhaps it always would.

Digging deep in the pocket of her jeans, Carrie found her paint rag, but mopping her eyes made her feel worse. With a gust of frustration she flung the rag on the floor. It was time to toughen up, and if just thinking about Nico made her cry and she thought about him all the time, she wouldn't think of him at all.

Until the next time.

She had avoided all newspapers like the plague, and she didn't have a clue what was happening in Niroli. Maybe Nico was engaged to Princess Anastasia by now. Now that he had proof he could father an heir, what was stopping him? He didn't have to resort to blackmail to keep Anastasia at his side, she was sure.

To avoid all complication she had cut herself off from her old life. She hadn't even given her new telephone number or address to Sonia at the office. Maybe she would one day, but not yet; there didn't seem any point. This wasn't just a few days out for her to lick her wounds; this was a new life. It was the only way she could think of to keep her baby safe.

Without Nico to organise security Carrie had come to the conclusion that the only way to ensure her baby's safety was to disassociate herself in every way from the richest royal family in the world. The decision to live in London wasn't ideal, but it had occurred to her that sometimes the best way to hide was in a crowd, and with all the galleries and offices she reasoned she'd have a better chance of earning a living in London than anywhere else.

The one thing that had turned out better than she had hoped was that her first paintings, created in a fever of heartbreak, had attracted more attention than she had dared to hope. Her preliminary sketches, along with the first painting she had completed, had received a favourable response from one of the smaller London galleries and now she was working on a collection for them, which she hoped to have finished before the busy Christmas-shopping season began.

She was an artist, a professional artist. It was all she had ever wanted.

Almost all…

Not nearly all…

Shaking herself out of it, Carrie picked up her palette knife and angled her head to view her latest creation. It showed purple and cerise bougainvilleas spilling down the palace walls… She had to grit her teeth to try and block out Nico and, still, it didn't work. There he was smack bang in the centre of her work. He was everything and everywhere; he always would be.

She painted on, finding a relief of sorts as she always did. She became absorbed and was oblivious to the thunder rolling overhead until the dark clouds gathering in sullen force stole her light away. Frowning, she stepped back from the canvas. Staring up at the gloomy sky, she concluded the weather wasn't about to improve anytime soon. Which meant it was as good an opportunity as any to replenish her paints. She worked so fast they ran out all the time….

Carrie didn't turn as the bell rang over the door of the small arts-and-craft shop. Why should she? She didn't know anyone in this part of London and no one knew her….

But there was something different in the air as the sound of the bell faded into silence. Something had changed, something fundamental, something that made all the tiny hairs rise on the back of her neck. And then she detected a strand of familiar scent on the musty air and, inhaling deeply, she let out the breath on a ragged sigh.

'Carrie?'

Clutching the countertop for support, she slowly turned around. 'How…' Her voice faded before she could say anything else. It must have been Nico's strength reaching out to her that stopped her sliding to the floor. He was dripping wet from the rain and had his collar turned up. He needed a shave and his jeans were soaked through. He looked exhausted, but…

'At last.' He gave her one of his crooked half-mocking smiles, stuffing the photograph he was carrying back in his pocket.

'How did you find me?' She felt as if she were suspended

in a net above the action, watching it, not taking part in it. She wanted to pinch herself to prove she wasn't dreaming, but didn't dare to move in case he disappeared.

'Your painting…' He sighed, exhaling long and slow with relief.

His voice strummed a long lost chord deep inside her that made her want to laugh and cry all at the same time.

His eyes were bright with triumph, with humour, and with something more she refused to see. 'But there are dozens of art shops in London….'

'Hundreds,' Nico assured her softly.

Carrie paid over her money in a trance. Nothing seemed real. Even taking hold of the bag with the tubes of paint and a bottle of linseed oil inside assumed a surreal quality.

'Let me take that for you—'

'No.' As Nico reached out to help her she clutched the paper bag to her chest. 'No, thank you, I can manage…' Manage? She could hardly exist in this strange situation. She wanted to get out of the shop and feel the rain on her face and still see Nico. Then she might believe he was here. His eyes were as bright as steel as he looked down at her, but it was impossible to read his thoughts. She could feel his aura… She could feel the energy coming off him and wrapping round her. She had to fight through it to get her own thoughts in order. Was he genuinely pleased to see her, or was it just the end of the chase? He had tried to blackmail her and she had eluded him. He hadn't changed that much. Nico would never let that pass…

And she didn't want any more pain in her life. That was her overriding feeling as they walked out of the shop. She couldn't go back to the constant humiliation and uncertainty. She didn't want to go back into a one-sided relationship. But neither could she bear to lose Nico again, Carrie thought, glancing up at him.

But what if his agenda hadn't changed? What if he still thought she was malleable and would do anything he asked… anything he ordered? But she couldn't keep running for ever. She wanted a happy life for her baby, and that meant a life with stability. She was going to settle down and call some place home, even if that home was a tiny apartment….

And then Nico sneezed, presenting her with a more immediate problem. 'You'd better come back to my place and dry off before you catch pneumonia.' Aware of how this might sound to him, she quickly modified, 'Or we could have a hot coffee somewhere?' But her cheeks were already on fire, giving away how much she loved him, how much she'd missed him, how much she cared for him.

'Good thinking,' he said lightly.

Crossing the road, he steered her towards the restaurant district where she took him to a local café, thinking the noise and bustle would cover any awkward silences between them. Beneath her excitement she was still wary, still vulnerable and she was frightened to read too much into his visit. Yes, he had gone to a lot of trouble finding her, but that didn't mean that Nico had suddenly developed a caring side to his nature. Nico simply couldn't accept defeat.

Buying two coffees for them, he secured seats by the window.

'I need you to come back to Niroli with me, Carrie.'

She was stunned. She couldn't believe Nico had launched straight in with that. He was acting as if they had never been apart. She was equally decisive with her answer. She told him no.

His gaze held hers. How could she have forgotten what it was like to be up against Nico's will when his engines were running on maximum revs? 'You tried to blackmail me into staying with you,' she reminded him. 'You can't do that, Nico, and you can't force me to come with you now.'

His gaze didn't waver. 'I'm here because we need to discuss the future of a baby.'

He had always known how to reach in and grab her heart. She would always put her baby first, and he knew that. 'Then, we'll talk here, in London.'

'No…' He shook his head, frowning as he straightened up. 'Something's come up. I have to get back to Niroli straight away—'

Carrie paled. 'Your mother—'

'My mother's fine. It's something else that won't wait.'

She would have heard if the king's health had deteriorated, Carrie thought, determined to hold her ground. 'My home is here in London, Nico.'

'If I could stay longer, I would. But I'm needed in Niroli.'

As he leaned across the table to stress the urgency of his commitment Carrie's thoughts flew immediately to Princess Anastasia. And she had done with playing second fiddle to Nico's prospective bride. She refocused as he started speaking again.

'My younger brother, Max, is struggling to control a vine crisis on the island and he badly needs my help…'

She felt guilty for thinking the worst of him, but after Nico's tactics in Niroli she had to be sure this wasn't another ploy.

'I'll do anything I can to help,' he continued, 'and I need to get back to him right away. I'm sorry, Carrie, but that's how it's got to be. I need your decision now. I can't wait.'

She guessed Nico had spent longer than he had intended looking for her. But this was typical of Nico; he was all business, all practicality. He was going to Niroli to help out his brother, but he would multi-task along the way, tying up the loose ends in his personal life. The baby was just another loose end and so was she. She had to wonder how he could be so matter-of-fact about a child that occupied her every waking thought. Maybe Nico couldn't imagine the moment he held his child in his arms for the first time; neither could she, but her heart was ready.

'You could have a full health check in Niroli,' he went on, instinctively homing into her weak spot again. 'Not to mention your first scan…' He looked at her expectantly.

'I've already got one booked, Nico. I'm going for it tomorrow—'

'I'd like to come with you….'

She stirred her coffee round and round, anything rather than look at him.

'Well?' he prompted. 'What do you think?'

Without raising her head, she told him the truth. 'I think that's a low blow, Nico. I think you play dirty.'

'When I have to,' he agreed.

She looked up at him then. 'And what will Princess Anastasia think of this arrangement?'

'What's it got to do with her?'

'Quite a lot, I'd say, if you're going to be married.'

'Married?'

As Nico grimaced she looked away. She didn't want to fuel the little bubble of hope inside her. It was always looking for an excuse to grow.

'Forget her, Carrie. Put Anastasia out of your mind. That's never going to happen.'

She was so relieved she almost threw her arms around his neck, but luckily she didn't and focused on her concern for his brother. 'I understand that you've got to return to Niroli.

Family must always come first. When this crisis at the vineyards is over, perhaps, we can talk then. Or do you intend to stay on in Niroli?' It was easier than asking him straight out if he was going to be King.

'My head office is in London,' he said without emotion.

'So, you'll be coming back here?'

'How about you, Carrie?' He asked rather than answered a question. 'Will you come back to work for me when the baby's older?'

'I don't know, Nico,' Carrie said honestly. She wouldn't rule anything out until she felt confident she could support her child. 'With the baby and now my painting, I don't know if I'll find it easy to work in an office again.'

'We'll miss you....'

Nico knew just how to pull her heartstrings. He had transformed everything she felt about him in the time it took to drink a cup of coffee. She pushed the cup away, reminding herself that Nico had blackmailed her and that was why she had run away from him. But he was making her want things like belonging somewhere, like being back in a familiar neighbourhood with friends around her, like having him around....

She tried hard not to stare at him when staring at him was all she wanted to do.

'You'll come back with me to Niroli and we'll talk?'

Nico's voice was so persuasive. And now she couldn't look away.

She should have remembered that he could never sit for long. When he stood she almost did, too, but then she remembered the fiasco at the banqueting hall and stopped herself just in time. 'You mean, you'll talk and I'll listen, Nico? That's not how it works; not anymore...'

'Then you'd better tell me how it does work.' Reaching into

his jacket pocket, he brought out a pen. Writing something on the back of the menu, he handed it to her. 'Here's my number. Call me when you're ready….'

He didn't wait to see her reaction.

As Carrie watched Nico ease his way through the closely packed tables she longed to chase after him. It was hard to believe he had gone to all this trouble to find her only to walk away. He didn't turn around once. Shouldering his way through the café door, he crossed the pavement and then jogged through the passing traffic to flag down a cab.

CHAPTER THIRTEEN

NICO, the consummate negotiator, Carrie thought as she paced up and down her small living room. He had given her no time to think, because he was only interested in a straight yes or no. Hadn't he said he could arrange a scan for her tomorrow in Niroli? He had probably flown to London in his private jet and might even have left the country by now….

But she had his mobile number on the back of the menu… She got through to him right away.

'I'll take a cab,' he said briskly, 'and pick you up on the way to the airport.'

'Thank you.' She barely managed that much before the line went dead.

Her appointment for a scan at the main hospital in Niroli was for late afternoon the following day. Having settled back into familiar surroundings at the palace, Carrie expected Nico might join her at some point during the day, but she saw him only twice, and then only through the window. The first time was barely minutes after they had arrived when he swept out in a hurry to see his brother, Max, and the second time was after lunch, when he appeared to be dressed for riding, judging by his breeches and casual shirt.

She felt a pang of jealousy as she watched him stride across the courtyard and then caught sight of herself in a mirror and laughed. Was she jealous of a horse now?

Carrie had thought that coming back to Niroli meant they would spend more time together, but Nico's schedule was squeezed into ever smaller boxes, and she hadn't found one with her name on it yet.

The next time she saw him was just before they had to leave for the hospital. She had been ready for ages and was waiting by the door. When the knock came she counted slowly to twenty before opening the door.

'Sorry this has to be quick,' Nico said, shouldering past her into the room.

'Don't worry, I'm ready….'

'No—' he shook his head, all rush and impatience '—I mean, there's hardly any time to give you this.' Digging into the pocket of his shirt, he brought out a box.

'What is it?'

'I realise this is hardly a romantic moment…' Grimacing, he shrugged and then glanced skywards as if divine intervention might be his only hope. 'It's a ring, Carrie….'

'A ring?' Her fingers tightened around the small black velvet box.

'An engagement ring,' Nico said as if that were obvious. 'Aren't you going to open it? Here—' he was as impatient as ever '—let me do it.' Peeling her fingers back, he removed the jewellery box from her hand, flipped it open and pulled out the biggest diamond Carrie had ever seen.

'Was this the biggest one in the shop?'

'Pretty much.' Nico's lips pressed down with concentration as he tried to force it on her finger.

'I meant was that your criteria for choosing it?' Carrie

didn't even glance at the egg-sized bauble that wouldn't make it past her first knuckle. She could just imagine the jeweller taking one look at a hunk like Nico, and, knowing he was the grandson of a king, picturing him with some supermodel with pin-thin fingers.

'I'm no good with jewellery…no practice…'

She should be grateful for that, Carrie supposed as Nico shot her his best winning smile. 'Nico, take it back,' she said, wrenching it from her finger. 'I don't want it.'

'You don't want it?' He sounded incredulous.

'You haven't listened to a word I've said to you, have you? I don't want to marry you and I don't want your money or what it buys. I don't want your status, either. I don't need it. I don't need any man to support me, or to present me with meaningless gifts.' Taking the box from him, Carrie carefully secured the ring in its slot. 'I'm sure you'll get your money back.'

'Don't worry about that—it's only on approval.'

'Well, that's great. I'm really pleased for you.'

At least he had the good grace to colour up.

'Carrie… I'm sorry, that was clumsy of me.'

'Yes, it was.' And this time, sorry wasn't enough. 'You managed to fit a little shopping into your lunch break, and you expect me to be grateful, is that it?' Her look was half sad, half wry. 'Marriage is a sacred pledge, Nico, and I don't want my baby growing up only to discover that the reason its parents married was because it was expedient at the time.'

'I thought we should firm things up—'

'Like signing a contract?'

'Exactly,' he said as if she'd seen the light.

Can't we at least pretend? Carrie bit down on the thought. Nico wanted to lay claim to her child, just in case, she knew that, but she didn't want to be a convenient womb for a man who didn't love her. She wanted to be loved for herself and she wanted to share the love inside her. A diamond, however big, meant less than nothing compared to that.

'Don't you want your child to be born in wedlock?'

He hadn't given up. But only because giving up wasn't in Nico's nature. 'I know plenty of single mothers who bring up children happily,' Carrie assured him, 'and the type of arrangement you're proposing won't make anyone happy, Nico. Don't kid yourself.'

'I just thought as a mother—'

She threw him a withering look. 'I'm sorry you have no understanding of how much a mother loves her children, particularly when you have such a wonderful mother yourself, a mother who clearly adores you and who would do anything in her power to secure your happiness. A legal document, just because it happens to be called a marriage certificate, won't make the slightest difference to the love a mother has for her child.'

Nico glowered at her, but at least he managed to hold himself in check. Opening the door for her, he stood aside. 'Come on, we'd better hurry, or we'll be late for your appointment at the hospital....'

Everything could change in a moment.

For both of them, Carrie realised. There had never been a more significant moment in her life than this, or anything close, and she knew without asking that Nico felt the same. She could feel his awe, his hope, excitement and his fear as they waited together, bound together more surely by this new life than they had ever been before.

The silent expectation of the technician, the flickering screen, the struggle to comprehend what they were seeing…

The hard hospital couch and cold jelly beneath the searching probe, Nico breathing steadily at her side, and her own breath hitching in her throat as she finally made out the tiny shape the radiographer was trying to explain to her… And then the sob that found its way from her throat at the moment that Nico exclaimed in wonder…

Every microsecond of that would be branded on her mind for all time.

'That's your baby,' the radiographer said.

'Yes, I know…' As Nico spoke he didn't move at all, he was transfixed by the screen. 'Can we have a print-off, please?'

'Certainly…'

As the radiographer made the necessary adjustments to her equipment Carrie turned her head away. She couldn't bear to see the look on Nico's face. She couldn't bear to see that and then have him, some time later, disillusion her. But it was already too late, she had already seen that he shared her feelings, but he didn't want to share her life and, for a moment, she almost wished he hadn't come with her.

No… No, she didn't mean that. How could she deny him this? But if he still doubted her, if he still doubted the tiny life growing inside her was part of him, then she didn't know if she could ever forgive him.

'Carrie… Carrie,' he said more insistently, 'look at this…'

Carried away by wonder and excitement, he helped her to sit up and then held the small photograph out in front of her.

'Can we keep it?' he said to the radiographer.

'Of course you can.' She smiled at him indulgently, as if she had lived this moment countless times before and had never tired of it.

'Don't cry, Carrie,' he said. 'It's wonderful.'

She closed her mind against all the things that Nico

couldn't see; all the things they could have shared together and never would. But when she opened her eyes again she saw with shock that Nico was crying, too…

He denied it, of course, when she pointed it out to him and then he stood up and made a performance of straightening the cuffs on his shirt. He looked too big for the room suddenly, too restless and awkward and eager to be gone and to be alone, to show his feelings to no one but himself.

'I'll leave you to get dressed.' He was already halfway through the door when the radiographer called him back.

'No, I'll go,' she said archly, 'and give you two some time together.'

'I…' Carrie's voice was lost in a flurry of activity and, before she knew it, the door had closed and she was alone with Nico.

'Incredible,' he murmured, still studying the photograph.

'Can I see?'

He tore his gaze away reluctantly. 'Yes, of course…'

Sitting down again at her side, he held it in front of her, refusing to relinquish hold of the image, giving the impression he would never let the small, grainy picture leave his possession again, not even for a second. 'Can you see this?' He angled the photograph. 'Do you think those are boy legs, or girl legs?'

'Does it matter? Do you care?' Carrie studied Nico's face. There was no chance she would distract him, not the slightest chance he would catch her staring at him….

'No, of course I don't care. As long as the baby's healthy, I don't mind if it's a girl or a boy.'

She had to smile at his confidence. He was determined to play a leading role in the upbringing of her baby, but quite how that was going to happen…

Fear of what Nico might do to keep her baby under his roof

drove her to hit back at him. 'But you won't know it's yours for another six months yet.'

And now the spell was broken. There had been no need to say that, but there were so many fears inside her competing with the joy and the fears had won.

'Don't you know yet?' he rebuked her softly.

'I know…'

She had to stop this agonising over everything Nico said, or might do, now or some time in the future, or anxiety would eat her up. The fact that he had stated his intention to be an effective parent was enough; she couldn't ask more of him.

'Do you mind if I keep this?' he said.

She wanted to tell him yes she did, but it seemed churlish when she had the baby.

'I'll get you a copy,' he said, still examining it.

'Will you?'

'You know I will.'

As their eyes met she believed him.

'I'll wait for you outside while you get dressed.'

The intimacy between them had disappeared, she realised as Nico left the room. The easy acceptance of their nakedness had vanished. They had shared this, the closest of moments, and yet something had died that would need rebuilding if they were ever to get it back again.

Nico said very little on the way back to the palace, and when they arrived he turned Carrie over to the care of his mother with little or no explanation other than the fact that he had to get back to his brother, Max, to finalise the plans they had been making. Anyone would be lucky to have Nico in their corner, Carrie reflected, standing back from the window so he wouldn't see her watching him as he left. He still had the photograph in his breast pocket, she realised. She wondered if he would get it out from time to time to take a look at it, or if he would be content just to keep it next to his heart.

She was dabbling her feet in the lake when he returned. She had just planted her hands on the cool grass behind her and was leaning back, closing her eyes. She didn't hear him at first and gave a little start when he hunkered down on the ground beside her. 'Is everything all right?' She shaded her eyes to look at him and was immediately concerned.

'Now it is,' he said, frustrating her desire to know more.

When he leaned across to brush a wing of hair from her face it was so unexpected that she flinched.

'Don't you trust me, Carrie?'

She held her breath.

'I'm sorry if I disturbed you.'

'You didn't disturb me.' But he was smiling at her in that way he had that made her heart perform somersaults.

'I was just admiring the view.'

'With your eyes closed?'

She had to smile.

'Let's do it together,' he suggested, leaning back and shutting his eyes.

'Nico…'

He opened one eye to look at her.

'You're impossible.'

'At last, we agree on something.'

He leaned closer, he leaned very close until she was sure he was going to kiss her, but instead he sprang to his feet, leaving her aching for him.

Walking away from her, he stood at the edge of the lake with his arms folded across his chest. 'So, how do you feel now, Carrie? Now you've seen the baby…'

She knew he'd walked away because he didn't want her to know how the scan had affected him.

'I feel wonderful,' she said honestly.

'And this isn't bad, is it?' His glance seemed to encompass everything: the view, the birdsong, the buzz of insects, the mellow summer breeze…

'White swans drifting on a silver lake? You're very lucky, Nico.' And when he didn't answer her, she patted the grass by her side. 'You can join me if you like.' His face was in shadow so she couldn't see what he was thinking, but after a few moments' hesitation he came to her.

As he settled down on the grass the gap between them closed slowly.

'When we had sex…you were a virgin?' he whispered.

'Yes, I was.'

It was almost as if some outside force had taken over where human feelings were insufficient. And when Nico kissed her this time it was very different. He kissed her in a way that was like a new beginning and made her yearn for him as she had never done before.

But then the doubt flooded back and she pulled away. Life couldn't be so cruel, could it?

'Where are you going?' Nico said, reaching out and capturing her wrist in one powerful fist.

She turned her face away from him. 'I couldn't bear this to be because you want to make me stay…' She turned back to him and held his gaze.

If he could only express his feelings… If he could only explain how he felt inside… He wanted her so badly, but the fierce compulsion to gratify his carnal urges had changed to something deeper. He drew her down to him very slowly and very carefully and, when she rested her arm above her head in an attitude of complete trust, his feelings took another giant leap. It was the same emotion he had felt during the scan and he recognised it now. It was the urge to love and protect someone and defend them with his life.

In the hospital he had been awestruck by Carrie's physical condition and by the sight of the tiny life growing inside her, and now he was simply awestruck by the strength of his feelings for her. He would do anything for her; he wanted nothing more than to show her homage as the mother of his child, nothing more than to make love to her, to really make love to her….

Raising himself on one elbow, he stared down. She looked so young, so vulnerable and, yet, she was so clearly aroused. Coiling a lock of her silky hair around his finger, he stroked it, loving the way it felt, so soft and clean between his fingers. Her fragrance drifted up to him, it was that wildflower scent he loved so much… It made him want to sink deep inside her and lose himself… It made him want to be part of her, to be part of her world.

'Aren't you going to kiss me, Nico?' she murmured softly.

If she only knew she could bring him to his knees with that cool blue stare. 'No,' he teased her back. 'I'm going to sit here and look at you. And then,' he added, when she pulled a face, 'I'm going to make love to you….'

As she sighed and softened in his arms the thought of making love to her in the open air was irresistible. Trailing his fingertips down the side of her neck, he brought them to the indentation where he loved to bury his tongue, and saw her quiver.

She couldn't resist him, she couldn't fight the longing inside her. Better women than she had been fools for love, Carrie reflected as Nico's fingertips trailed fire up and down her arms. When he lifted his hands away she moved closer to him, she couldn't help herself. Sliding his hand down her arm, he laced his fingers through her fingers, joining them in a way that made her yearn to be closer still.

'Shall I kiss you?' he suggested, brushing her lips with his mouth. 'Would you like that, Carrie?'

'Do you expect me to answer that?'

He deepened the kiss slowly, barely touching her with his hands. She was so comfortable on her grassy bed and the light was gentle. The only sound disturbing them was the call of the turtle doves and even that was muted. But as she lay safe in Nico's arms, Carrie shivered as if a dark cloud passed over them. Making love in the open air was exciting, but not without risk of discovery, and the fact that Nico knew no boundaries frightened her.

CHAPTER FOURTEEN

NICO GAVE Carrie no time to think before catching her to him and kissing her deeply, pressing her to the ground with renewed urgency. It was an urgency that infected them both. Wrapping her arms around him, she drew him closer still, loving the warm, firm touch of him beneath her hands, and very soon she was drowning in that warmth and in Nico's clean, familiar scent. 'Are you sure no one will see us?'

'They might hear us… In fact, there's a good chance they will.'

'I'm being serious, Nico,' Carrie warned him.

'You can make as much noise as you like,' he promised her.

'What makes you think I want to?'

'I know you do… I know you will…'

He smiled against her mouth, and she was lost from that moment on. Her mind knew nothing but Nico… Nico's scent, his touch, his voice… He was going to make love to her; this time Nico was really going to make love to her.

But then he surprised her, as he always could, pulling back, holding her at arm's length to smile his irresistible smile into her eyes. 'I've just thought of something.'

'What?'

'This is your chance to walk naked through the water like a nymph. You wouldn't miss out on that, would you?'

'The cold water,' Carrie reminded him, staring at the tranquil surface of the lake. 'After you…' She should have known better. Nico didn't hesitate. Stripped naked in seconds, he turned away from her and dived in.

'Take your clothes off and join me,' he challenged, treading water.

Carrie gazed around anxiously. She followed him tentatively, arms crossed against her body. As she had expected the water was freezing. It was all or nothing. Ducking her head beneath the surface, she rose up, spluttering and exclaiming with shock, before launching herself into a vigorous breaststroke.

Nico didn't seem to notice how cold the water was as he sculled lazily by her side. His powerful arms sliced through the water with no effort at all and, when they reached the shallows, he reached out and pulled her to him. 'That's far enough,' he said, putting his hands round her waist to hold her close to him.

Their lips were touching as he lifted her and her legs were weightless. Before she knew it they were wrapped around his waist.

The water was her pillow and as she leaned back she gasped as Nico sank deep inside her. Did sensation come any more extreme than this? The chill of the water surrounding her and the heat of Nico inside her….

The lake undulated around them as they began to move. It cooled them and supported them as they became lost in the grip of pleasure, wrapped in each other's arms. And when she was exhausted Nico carried her back to shore. Laying her gently on the ground, he made this pledge against her lips: 'Next time in bed, Carrie.' And then he laughed softly as if that in itself would be an adventure.

'Do you think?' Carrie murmured sleepily. She had never felt so content, or so relaxed. And it was all because she felt secure and certain that Nico had changed. He had changed for all of them, but especially for his child.

They spent the whole night together. And in bed, as Nico pointed out to Carrie with amusement…

When she woke it was to find Nico with his face turned towards her on the pillows. Smiling drowsily, she sighed with contentment as he laced his fingers through her hair and allowed it to fall in a shimmering cascade around her shoulders.

'I love you so much,' she murmured, reaching for him. Linking her arms around his neck, she drew him close, but was disappointed to feel him already restless. 'Can't we spend the whole day in bed?' she begged seductively.

'Another time, *bellissima…*'

The way Nico spoke to her broke the mood in tiny pieces. In a rush all of Carrie's insecurities returned. Nico didn't love her. He loved his mouse, the cute little pet in his mind that was always there at his beck and call. To think anything else was crazy.

But even pride wasn't enough to stop her asking him, 'Can't you stay a bit longer?' She badly needed a cuddle, some reassurance… But then she remembered his brother, Max, and the concern that had brought Nico racing to his brother's side. 'I'm sorry, I had forgotten—'

'Forgotten what?' he said, leaning up on one elbow to stare down at her.

'I'd forgotten your brother Max.'

'Oh, yes,' he said, relaxing down again. For barely a minute.

Carrie was sitting up in bed when Nico returned back from the shower. 'I'll see you later?' She wanted an answer. The shadow that had been hovering over them the previous evening seemed to have settled on the room.

'Of course you will,' Nico said distractedly, easing riding breeches over his muscular thighs.

'Are you going riding today?' A silly question, but she hoped to prompt him into saying more.

Nico's reply was a faint smile.

'Stay safe.'

'You know I will,' he said with his usual confidence. And then he came to her side to say goodbye, but he only dropped a kiss on his fingers and placed them on her lips.

'You're not planning to take any risks, are you?' She couldn't stop herself and was already braced to receive his impatient stare.

'No.'

What made him glance at her belly? He looked so tense she didn't know if she could believe him. Reaching up, she stroked his face. The stubble was so rough and black even now when he'd just had a shave. It made him look dangerous and tough, and the knowledge that he liked to test himself made dread rise like bile in her throat. 'Nico, what are you planning?'

'Planning?'

He refused to answer that and took hold of her hand instead. Bringing it to his lips, he kissed her fingertips, but she could tell that he was distracted. In his mind he had already left her, Carrie realised.

She had wondered about all the flags and bunting strung from the castle battlements. When Princess Laura explained the reason for them Carrie's earlier sense of dread increased. They were in honour of the Palio, the annual horse race through the old city. Men with loyalties to different ancient families gathered to pit themselves and their horses against each other. It was both exciting and dangerous to watch, Princess Laura had said, and so they would stand on the ramparts where they were certain to be safe from flying hooves.

Apparently, the racetrack circled the main square and then wove through the narrow streets, which gave the crowds a grandstand view. The riders took far too many risks, Princess Laura had told her, because there was a lot at stake. The reward for the winner was nothing more than an old flag, but the real prize was honour and for that, men would risk their lives, she'd added with an accepting shrug.

Nico's was an ancient family, Carrie thought anxiously, the most ancient of all the families in Niroli. But, surely, he wouldn't be involved? She had asked the princess, who had dismissed the idea out of hand, saying she would never allow a son of hers to take part in the Palio; it was far too dangerous.

That had been the cue for Carrie's heart to thump with alarm, and now she was alone in her room she could think of nothing else. How many years had it been since Nico had obeyed a direct order from his mother? She had almost worn a hole in the rug fretting about him. He had been wearing riding breeches when he had left her; what was she supposed to think? And how could he take part in such a dangerous race when he knew he was soon to be a father?

He wouldn't, Carrie assured herself. Nico might not love her sufficiently to tell her where he was going, but he would never take part in the Palio now he had discovered he had a child on the way.

She was overcome with relief when he returned unexpectedly and followed him to the bathroom, watching him like a hawk as he sluiced his face, trying to detect the smallest clue that might point to him preparing for the race. But then she remembered that danger was commonplace for Nico and there would be no clues.

'I'm sorry, am I intruding on your afternoon?' he demanded mockingly when she hovered anxiously at his side.

'Just tell me you wouldn't—'

'Wouldn't what?' Nico cut across her. His voice was muffled as he dried his face.

'You wouldn't expose yourself to danger?'

Straightening up, he tossed the towel over the rail. 'I'm not the one who's pregnant, Carrie. I don't have to sit with my feet up all day—'

'And neither do I, Nico. And you know that's not what I am talking about.'

'What are you talking about? What's on your mind, Carrie?'

'Are you going to race in the Palio?'

'And if I am?'

'And if I don't want you to?' She was forced to move back as he moved past her into the bedroom.

'I'd say you'd have to rethink.'

His manner frightened her. 'Is that why you brought me back to Niroli, Nico…to watch you kill yourself?'

'I came back to Niroli for my brother; the race is an incidental—'

'An incidental?' Carrie interrupted. 'Like me? Like your baby? Or do we come even lower down in the pecking order than the race?'

'Carrie, stop this,' he snapped.

She shrugged him off when he tried to take hold of her. 'I think you're in love with danger. I think it's the only thing you do love. And that makes me wonder, Nico, what small part of your heart is left for me and how much for your baby—'

'Now you're overreacting and being ridiculous—'

'Am I? Is it ridiculous to love someone as much as I love you?'

'It's only a horse race—'

'A dangerous horse race!' She cut across him. 'A horse race like no other!'

'You have been doing your homework.'

'Don't mock me and don't turn away from me!' Chasing after him, she grabbed his sleeve before he reached the door. 'I love you, Nico… Please don't do this…' His arm was stiff and unresponsive beneath her hand; his face no less so.

'I'm not ten years old, Carrie.' He snatched his arm from her grasp. 'Stay out of things you don't understand. The Palio is a matter of national pride—'

'The Palio is a battle of testosterone!'

'Spoken like a woman—'

'Spoken like the mother of your child! The mother who wants a father for her child…' It was pointless trying to reason with him, Carrie realised. 'You haven't changed, at all, have you, Nico?'

'I'm sorry if I disappoint you—'

'Just don't expect to find me on the sidelines, cheering you on.'

'I don't expect anything of you,' he assured her. 'That way I can never be disappointed.'

Carrie went cold. Nico had just made it plain that her love meant nothing to him. There was no point trying to stop him as he turned and walked away.

The old city had come alive with banners and bands and sideshows and food stalls. Carrie had never seen anything like it before. She had slipped away from the palace after making her excuses to Princess Laura, telling a small lie, saying the heat was too much for her and she was retiring to her room.

The heat? That was the least of it. Her heart was thundering above the noise of the crowd and all she could think about was finding Nico. It didn't matter how little he thought of her, she had to try and stop him risking his life.

One of the footmen had told her that Nico would be in the old town by now. The boy had smiled broadly as he'd told her, as if hinting at some extraordinary exploit. That was all she had needed to fuel her anxiety. She had returned to her room right away and slipped into a summer dress, because she knew the heat inside the walled town would be stifling. She was going to find out where the race started from and if Nico was there she would beg him, if she had to, not to take part.

When she reached the centre there was a fever in the air adding to the impression that this was a modern-day gladiatorial race without all the usual regulations and safeguards for the jockeys. She couldn't let Nico ride….

Carrie could smell the horses before she saw them. She could smell the acrid stench of their sweat, mixed with hot leather and the sweet smell of fear.

Squeezing her way between some food stalls, she managed to push her way to the front of the crowd. People had gathered around a group of nervy thoroughbreds that had been contained in a small roped-off area. Handlers clung on desperately to bridles and lead ropes as the horses bucked and shimmied around the small ring. And then she realised it was a bareback race, the most dangerous race of all.

But Nico wasn't anywhere to be seen. Turning back, Carrie had to force her way through the crowd. She went back into the vast square in which the race would be run. It sloped inwards like the hub of a great wheel and was paved with slippery stones that made every step treacherous. How much more so for a horse's hooves? More specifically for the hooves of Nico's horse? The thought of him travelling the dangerous route at breakneck speed brought on a fresh wave of panic.

She could see the track was being covered in sand, which would offer the horses some protection, but it was narrow and had turns so sharp she could only imagine the jockeys would have to wheel their horses around at right angles. And there surely wasn't room for two horses to race side by side… Standing on tiptoe, Carrie tried to see over the crowd. She hadn't come this far to be beaten now. She might not speak Nirolian, but a person's name was universal…

'Nico Fierezza?' An elderly woman turned to face Carrie as she shouted out Nico's name. The old lady nodded with approval. 'I know him. Nico Fierezza is riding for my family.'

Carrie's heart contracted with fear and then reason kicked in. 'Your family?' Surely, that couldn't be right? The old lady was from the countryside where they still wore traditional dress. It seemed unlikely she could be a relative of Nico's.

'Yes, for my family,' the woman insisted proudly, tapping her chest. 'We have never won the Palio, but Nico has offered to ride for us today and Nico will win.'

Carrie was too full of emotion to speak for a moment. Nico was so much better and so much worse than she thought him. 'Do you know where I can find him?'

'Yes, of course, he will be at the starting rope now. He will be there for my family,' the old lady said again with great pride.

'Can I go to him?'

As the woman looked at Carrie her face softened. 'You will be my guest,' she said. 'But we will wait for him at the winning post. We will be the first to greet him when he rides over the line.'

'Oh, no, I must see him now…' But the old lady didn't hear

her, and the next thing Carrie knew she was being shepherded along. She tried again, but her voice was drowned out by the sound of church bells tolling. It seemed that every bell in Niroli had started up in competition with her.

'The bells won't stop until the race begins,' the old lady yelled in Carrie's ear. 'The bells are ringing because the horses in the race are being blessed.'

'In the churches?' Carrie looked at her in astonishment.

'In many churches, all over the city.' The woman beamed. 'And now you and I shall go to my family's quarters.'

'Oh, no, I…' Carrie didn't want to go anywhere but to Nico, but the woman insisted on dragging her along and was in no mood to listen.

When they arrived Carrie was relieved to find that the 'quarters' of each family was simply a place in the square marked by a flag. Tables at least forty yards long were lined up and each of them was loaded with food and jugs of wine.

'This is our rehearsal for the victory celebration,' the elderly woman told her now, seeing Carrie's curiosity as she stared at the people already eating and drinking. 'The Palio is blood, noise and hysteria, for which we need plenty of fuel.'

As she cackled her approval Carrie blenched. She had seen the track with its hair-raising turns. She had come to accept that she couldn't change Nico, and maybe she shouldn't try, but this was far too dangerous.

'Jockeys have been known to be killed…horses, too…'

'Killed…' Where was he? Carrie wondered in an agony of concern as the old lady continued her litany of doom. Nico had to pull out of the race. He had to… She stared around desperately. There seemed to be more people than ever in the square, and Princess Laura had explained that more than thirty thousand would crowd into the city that day.

Carrie was sure they were all here now, pressing in on her. A wave of nausea swept over her...a warning. The heat was stifling. And on top of that there was the raging inferno of competition. The noise, the barely suppressed violence... Carrie could identify the rival families by the different colours they wore, and the atmosphere was growing more aggressive by the minute. She was jostled as some members of the crowd started heckling, while their opponents cheered their favourites... But Nico...where was Nico?

Heated words were exchanged right next to her as several jockeys rode past. Carrie's heart was thundering with fear. She should never have done this; emotion could turn so quickly to blows. But she was trapped in the crowd, trapped by desperation to find Nico before it was too late. Determined to keep her baby safe, she squeezed her way through to a quieter spot behind some barriers. She could see the riders streaming past... But she couldn't see Nico... She shivered to see the expression on the faces of the men. They all looked the same, like tough, hard, fighting men who would show each other no mercy.

And then, by some miracle, he was right in front of her. She thrust out her arms and cried out his name to attract his attention, but he rode past without seeing her. His mount was skittish, jibbing from the howls of the crowd, and it was taking all his concentration to prevent it from rearing up. He looked darker and more forbidding than she had ever seen him. Naked to the waist, his face grimly set in an expression of absolute determination. His thighs were like a steel vise around the stallion's flanks, and Carrie didn't have the slightest doubt that Nico was more than a match for the other men. But the fact that he was here at all and taking part in such a ferocious, unforgiving battle terrified her. She called out to him again and waved her arms frantically in the hope he might see her, but the crowd was too noisy and he didn't turn around, and she could only watch in desperation as he rode away.

'Three times round the race track…'

'What?' Carrie clutched her throat as she turned to face the elderly woman at her side.

'Three times round the race track. You must come with me,' she insisted, 'so we can be at the winning post to cheer him on.'

The whole crowd was moving and Carrie found it impossible to resist the flood of humanity at her back. She was glad of the older woman's hand on her arm, directing her, but who knew where…

Using elbows and determination they finally reached the winning post and secured a prime position. 'When will the race begin?' Carrie said, taking advantage of a rare hush. But her companion's answer was superfluous; the roar of the crowd told her everything. Noise exploded into the silence with such ferocity it shook the ground beneath her feet. Shutting her eyes, Carrie knew the only thing left to her was to wish Nico safe with every fibre of her being.

Two minutes, fifty-two seconds…that was the record; she'd seen it in the archives kept at the palace. One hundred and ninety-two seconds, and she already knew that each one of them would feel like an hour.

Leaving the shelter of the elderly woman's side, Carrie pushed her way to the front of the crowd. She had to see him… She had to be the first to know that Nico was safe… She had to count the horses in one by one… She didn't care if Nico won, or if he came last, she just wanted to see him cross the line safely….

CHAPTER FIFTEEN

MORE PEOPLE crowded in to see the last lap. It was easy to mark the progress of the race thanks to the waves of noise and the shouts of the crowd. Carrie couldn't see the horses yet; she couldn't see anything but heads, shoulders and backs. The crowd was pressing in on her as people grew increasingly excited. The heat was extraordinary… There was no air left to breathe, no wind to cool her.

She could see them! Nico was safe! She could see him and his nearest rival, neck and neck… Well clear of the following group, they were thundering towards her. She could smell them now; she could smell the tang of violent struggle. The noise was tremendous and sparks flashed off the ancient cobbles beneath the stallion's hooves. Nico was lying flat on his mount's sweating neck… The horse was grimacing with effort, ears back, teeth exposed in his frothing muzzle and the whites of his eyes showing clear round the ebony globes.

Her head was thumping, pounding, people screaming in her ears. Firecrackers erupted in the sky as the end drew close… Streamers flew behind the horses' heads like flames of red and gold…two stallions tearing towards her, muscles straining to the limit. They were so close she could see their nostrils flaring, and then there was only terror and heat and the press of people at her back… Stumbling forwards, she tried to regain her balance and failed. She didn't know what was happening, only that her knees gave way beneath her and then she was falling, falling…

And somehow, incredibly, she was safe in Nico's arms. His voice brought her back. He was calling to people to make way for them as he carried her through the crowd. So many things flashed in front of her eyes. She couldn't make sense of any of it… There was noise banging in her head, and Nico, Nico holding her as if she were the most precious thing on earth to him… And then the darkness closed over her again.

'No…no…' She pushed the cup away, shaking her head with distress. Nico was trying to make her drink something. 'I've ruined it for you… Oh, Nico, I'm so sorry…' As she saw the older woman who had befriended her hovering anxiously in the background Carrie's pain increased; she had spoiled the day for so many people.

'*Cara mia,* have I hurt you?'

Nico had mistaken her distress for pain and was looking at her with such concern in his eyes she explained to him all in a rush that it wasn't him who had hurt her, but her own foolishness.

'You were looking for me,' he reminded her tenderly. 'This is all my fault. I left you in such uncertainty, who could blame you? Certainly not me, *carissima,*' he assured her. 'I can only thank God you're safe. I can't believe I nearly lost you—' He buried his face in her arms.

'You saved my life, Nico. You risked your life to save me….'

'I love you,' he said, raising his head to stare her in the eyes. 'What else would I do? If you had been killed my life would be over.'

'You love me?' Struggling upright, Carrie stared at him. 'You love me?' she repeated softly.

'When you stumbled out from the crowd my whole life flashed in front of me, and it was a life without you, Carrie.'

'But I ruined everything for you.' She stared at him, stared at the familiar, beloved face etched with pain. 'You lost the race because of me…'

'The race?' Nico stared at her, his eyes clouded with bewilderment as if he had forgotten the race. 'You were all I saw… You, Carrie. You filled my mind… A world without you…' He shook his head. 'Have you any idea what that would be like?' His voice was hoarse with emotion as he stared at her.

'But the Palio—'

Nico stopped her, putting a finger over her lip. 'Nothing…nothing is more important to me than you, and I nearly lost you.' He dragged her close.

'People are cheering, calling your name. Nico—' Carrie pulled back to stare at him '—what's happening? I don't understand….'

'What can you remember about the race?' he prompted gently.

Carrie shook her head and sighed. It was so hard to remember anything, and now Nico was dropping passionate kisses on her neck, it was impossible. But she tried, for his sake, she tried. The horses had been charging straight at her… She had stumbled into their path… After that…

'I must have fainted…' And if she had fainted then Nico must have leapt from his galloping horse to save her. Carrie went very still. Before he could reply the old lady who had befriended her came forward to see how she was. There were more people, crowding behind her; her family, Carrie guessed.

She was instantly paralysed with guilt and shame to think her fainting had cost them the race. 'I'm so sorry…'

'Sorry?' the old woman exclaimed. 'You should be happy you have won the heart of the winner of the Palio.'

Carrie turned to Nico in bewilderment. 'What does she mean?'

'She means I won,' he said with his usual economy of words and emotion.

'You won?' He was so matter-of-fact, the change in him was stark. When he had professed his love for her he had shown more feeling than this. 'I don't understand how you could have won the race when you didn't cross the line. What? Why are you smiling at me, Nico?'

'Should a winner be sad?'

'You won the Palio?' Carrie shook her head, still not understanding.

'I won your heart,' he said, and as Nico stared at her Carrie felt his intensity and his need for her to believe him.

'Yes, you did,' she said softly, 'but because of me you lost the race. You don't have to pretend otherwise to try and make me feel better.'

'Have I ever lied to you, Carrie?'

'Never.' It was true; he never had.

'Then, believe me when I tell you that I won the Palio. Or should I say, my horse won the Palio.' He stroked her face very gently, smoothing away the concern. 'Fuoco's headpiece was in place when he crossed the line, which is all that matters. No one cares about the jockey.'

'I do,' Carrie declared passionately.

'Then, you're on your own,' Nico assured her, with a wry smile. 'It's enough to know that Fuoco won the Palio.'

As he spoke a cheer went up making further conversation impossible and Carrie's heart soared as she gazed at all the glowing faces gathered around them. 'I'm just so proud of you.'

'And I'm just so relieved you're safe, *piccolo topo*.'

She could see by his face he was teasing her. 'What does that mean?'

'Little mouse,' Nico admitted dryly.

They were distracted by the sound of a resounding splash and some good-natured jeering.

'Feel sorry for him,' Nico said by way of explanation.

'Sorry for whom?'

'For the jockey who came second. He's been pitched into the horse trough for his trouble.'

'But if he came second he did really well.' Considering the competition, he must have ridden extremely well, Carrie thought proudly, staring at Nico.

'Here in Niroli second place is considered more shameful than coming last,' he explained. 'If you come second the belief is that you could have won if you had only tried a little harder.'

'Well, I'm glad you were saved a soaking,' Carrie said, nestling deeper into Nico's embrace.

'So am I… Though there were the odd moments when I doubted that I would…'

And now she doubted he was talking about the Palio. 'Do you still have doubts?'

'None,' Nico assured her. 'Now I am absolutely certain.'

And as cheers rose all around them for the hero, Nico Fierezza, who had won the Palio for the underdogs Nico drew his beloved Carrie into his arms and kissed her.

They were back at the palace where Nico had insisted Carrie must rest. He had called for a doctor, who had pronounced her fit and well, but said she was a victim of the heat that affected so many at this time of year. Nico had enforced his will on this occasion and had Carrie propped up on a daybed on a balcony overlooking the lake.

'There must be no more skydiving from ridiculous heights,' she told him, 'no more diving with sharks, or dicing with death on white-water rapids and no more horse races—'

'And how shall I change you?' he said, pretending to ponder the dilemma.

Nico's eyes were dark as sleep and Carrie felt a stirring of fear, knowing that he courted danger as assiduously as most people avoided it. She couldn't bear to think about the possibility of losing him and had to know he would give up his love affair with extreme sports. 'I'm being serious, Nico. You must promise me now that you're going to be a father all risk-taking will stop.'

'Then shall I leave you?'

'No… And don't tease me,' Carrie warned him, 'because this is serious.'

'It's easy to take risks when you have no one dependent on you,' Nico observed.

'No one's dependent on you now,' Carrie assured him, 'but that doesn't mean to say you can take risks.'

'So is this a one-way relationship?' Nico mocked her gently. 'Maybe you don't want to be dependent on me, Carrie, but our child will have to be dependent on both of us. And it wouldn't be so bad if you were dependent on me, too, would it?' There was a serious question in his eyes.

'You know my position and it hasn't changed.'

'Would your position remain the same if we were married?'

Carrie went very still as Nico added, 'It makes sense, you know it does. You can depend on me to take care of you and still retain your independence.'

And when she still didn't speak he went on, 'I want to look after you, Carrie. I want to shoulder full responsibility for you and for the baby.'

'And you're sure that's not just duty speaking?' She would rather remain on her own than have Nico stand by her out of a sense of duty.

'I'm quite sure.' Coming to kneel by her daybed, Nico took her hand and, resting it briefly against his brow, he brought it to his lips and pressed a kiss on her palm. 'Say you'll marry me, Carrie…'

Say you'll make me a father… It was too late. All the old doubts and insecurities had flown back into her mind. She was plain and she was dull, and Nico was…

'Getting married makes good sense, you know it does,' he tried again, unaware of her inner turmoil.

Sense? She had used good sense all her life, except where Nico was concerned, and she never wanted to use good sense where love was concerned. 'I don't want to—'

'Carrie, please…'

She turned her face away from him. She wanted more than a cold-blooded arrangement based on good sense; she wanted Nico with his guard down, she wanted a proposal of marriage from a man who loved her to distraction. What she didn't want was another business proposition. 'I need time to think, Nico… And now I need to sleep.' Which was a lie. It was the last thing she needed. 'The heat…' She made a weak gesture with her hand.

'Of course…'

Carrie didn't turn to look as Nico walked away. Had she ruined everything? Nico had proposed marriage and she had refused him a second time. He had told her that he loved her and she had turned him away.

Because his emotions were on fire, he wasn't thinking rationally… She had to think for him. He had been caught up in the passion of the Palio, and then in her near accident. And if he loved her at all it was because she was carrying his longed-for child….

Crunching up her fingers, Carrie pressed them against her forehead, wishing it could be different. Everything Nico had said to her should have been enough, but the recognition that it was adrenalin driving him meant it wasn't enough and never could be. She couldn't accept him. A marriage without love was no marriage at all, and a loveless marriage to Nico would destroy her.

He'd had a night to sleep on what had happened and he still found it hard to believe that he had handled the situation so badly. In business he was always sure-footed, he always knew the right thing to say, but when it came to personal relationships he was out of his depth.

Using business terminology—contracts, good sense—was hardly the right language to use when he was speaking to the love of his life about the most important decision they would ever make. He'd made so many mistakes. First he'd tried to blackmail Carrie into staying with him and then he'd risked his life knowing he was going to be a father. No wonder she thought he didn't care about her or their baby. She was too shrewd to be steamrollered and he was going to lose her if he wasn't careful.

He was so used to having everything his own way he hadn't prepared for the possibility that Carrie might refuse his proposal of marriage. But on the plus side, he didn't know what it was to give up, either.

* * *

Carrie hugged herself as she stared out across the lake. The smooth sheet of water had turned rosy gold in the early evening light and was lit with fiery lanterns in honour of a small ceremony to mark the end of the Palio. There would be a reception, Nico had told her, which he hoped she would attend.

She would leave then to start her new life. It seemed appropriate to be leaving Nico in the midst of victory—one of his many victory celebrations.

The only victory Carrie cared about was hearing Nico tell her that he loved her, that he really loved her. Perhaps she was more needy than most. She had felt so lonely with her aunt and realised now it must have affected her. But the loneliness she had experienced then was nothing compared to this, Carrie thought as she turned away from the lake. Leaving Nico again was the hardest thing she'd ever have to do. She could see everything she had done wrong. She had tried to change him…but into what? Wasn't he the man she had fallen in love with?

Even in her present mood she couldn't help smiling when she saw him coming across the grass towards her. It was tempting to believe her thoughts had summoned him and, because she couldn't wait to find out what he wanted, she ran to meet him.

'You should be resting,' he said with concern. Taking hold of her arms, he drew her in front of him.

'Nico, I'm sorry.'

'For what? Carrie…for what?'

'For trying to change you. Can we stay as we are? Can we be friends? I know I shouldn't try to change you any more than you should try to change me. Will you forgive me, Nico?'

'Slow down… What are you talking about?'

It was the most she had said in a long time, and as words

never came easily to her, she had used them all up and could only shake her head at him now.

'I'm in no hurry,' Nico said gently, 'Take your time and tell me what's wrong. What's upset you?'

'It's not enough to be married to you, Nico,' she finally managed. 'I want to be loved….'

His beautiful blue-grey eyes darkened. 'And do you think I don't love you?'

'You've never said so…except after the race, and that was different—'

'Different? Why?'

'You were upset and shocked…we both were.'

She was right about that. And what she didn't know was that words didn't come easily to him, either, which was why he had always felt close to her. He was capable of strong feelings, but expressing them…that, he found impossible. He could tease her, he could make light of anything, but expressing his love for her… 'I love you, Carrie.' He looked deep into her eyes. 'I've always loved you and I will always love you. You're my one love, you're my life, you're the air I breathe, my world, my whole existence. Please say you'll marry me and spend your life with me so that I can try to make you as happy as you make me…'

'Nico…' She looked at him, wanting him to say the words he'd just said over and over again.

'I loved you from the first moment I saw you, I just didn't know it at the time.'

As his face creased into the familiar smile, she wrapped her arms around his neck and held him close.

'And now we've got a party to go to,' he reminded her, gently disentangling himself.

'A party?' She didn't want to go to a party. She wanted to

stay with Nico and hear him tell her he loved her a thousand times more.

'The reception I told you about?' he prompted. 'And maybe we could think about celebrating our engagement at the same time….'

'But I haven't even said yes, yet,' Carrie pointed out.

'But you will,' Nico said confidently.

She felt as if she were floating, or maybe walking on air. Nico had made the announcement of their engagement formally in front of his whole family. King Giorgio had surprised them by saying there were some things that even a king couldn't change and that love was one of them. He'd wished them both well and said he looked forward to the birth of a great-grandchild. Princess Laura was ecstatic and promised to come and visit them frequently in London.

'You must come very soon,' Nico had said, proudly tightening his hold on Carrie's waist, 'My wife-to-be has an exhibition pending of her paintings.'

This reminded Carrie of her gift she had brought with her for Nico's mother and so she excused herself and ran back to her apartment to collect the painting she had completed…the painting of Princess Laura's private garden.

'My secret garden,' Princess Laura exclaimed with delight when Carrie handed it to her.

'Not so secret anymore, Mother,' Nico told her dryly. 'The gallery owners have chosen this image for the front of Carrie's programme.'

The princess was delighted, and even King Giorgio was impressed. As for Carrie, the only thought in her head was Nico. She'd have to paint him… But first she would have to find a way to make him stand still.

'Why are you smiling?' he said, drawing her aside.

'Because I'm in love with the most infuriating man on earth.'

'That's good,' he said.

'Good?' she said, frowning as she looked up at him.

'I can't bear coming second,' he told her dryly, pulling her close.

'No more competitions, Nico,' Carrie implored him. 'I couldn't bear it. You don't understand. I've never had so much to lose before—'

'You're enough danger for me,' Nico assured her, sweeping her into his arms in front of everyone present. 'When I wasn't looking, Mother Mouse grew teeth, so I know to be on my guard.'

'And you're pleased about that?'

'What do you think?' he said, sharing a private look with her.

'For ever?' She searched his face.

'You know I thrive on challenge….'

* * * * * *

As the search for a ruler of Niroli continues
and another Fierezza male relinquishes the throne,
a world away another man is left with little choice....

'ALL that I have is yours.' His brother's eyes snapped up to meet his steely gaze. 'Take care of it. Take care of them. I trust you to be their leader.'

He wasn't a man of many words, so when he spoke, people listened. Beneath his bequest his brother could read a thousand thoughts. They both knew what had happened. They both knew it was time for him to leave. His brother would take care of his people. He had been snapping at his heels for a lifetime, desperate for the role. His mind and his soul were honed for the challenge. There were impressive footsteps to follow but he trusted he would fill them well. His brother wasn't a born ruler, but then, few men were....

The few that were knew they were, and this one was about to leave to claim a new life, a new kingdom, a new title.

'Look after my people, I must go.'

* * * * *

*And so the desert sheikh prepares to leave
the kingdom he was born to rule.
But a new kingdom needs him more.
Don't miss THE PRINCE'S FORBIDDEN VIRGIN
to discover more!*

SPECIAL EDITION®

Life, Love and Family

*These contemporary romances will strike a chord with you
as heroines juggle life
and relationships on their way to true love.*

New York Times *bestselling author Linda Lael Miller
brings you a BRAND-NEW contemporary story
featuring her fan-favorite McKettrick family.*

Meg McKettrick is surprised to be reunited with her high
school flame, Brad O'Ballivan. After enjoying a career
as a country-and-western singer, Brad aches for a home
and family...and seeing Meg again makes him realize he
still loves her. But their pride manages to interfere with
love...until an unexpected matchmaker gets involved.

*Turn the page for a sneak preview of
THE McKETTRICK WAY by Linda Lael Miller
On sale November 20, wherever books are sold.*

Brad shoved the truck into gear and drove to the bottom of the hill, where the road forked. Turn left, and he'd be home in five minutes. Turn right, and he was headed for Indian Rock.

He had no damn business going to Indian Rock.

He had nothing to say to Meg McKettrick, and if he never set eyes on the woman again, it would be two weeks too soon.

He turned right.

He couldn't have said why.

He just drove straight to the Dixie Dog Drive-In.

Back in the day, he and Meg used to meet at the Dixie Dog, by tacit agreement, when either of them had been away. It had been some kind of universe thing, purely intuitive.

Passing familiar landmarks, Brad told himself he ought to turn around. The old days were gone. Things had ended badly between him and Meg anyhow, and she wasn't going to be at the Dixie Dog.

He kept driving.

He rounded a bend, and there was the Dixie Dog. Its big neon sign, a giant hot dog, was all lit up and going through its corny sequence—first it was covered in red squiggles of light, meant to suggest ketchup, and then yellow, for mustard.

Brad pulled into one of the slots next to a speaker, rolled down the truck window and ordered.

A girl roller-skated out with the order about five minutes later.

When she wheeled up to the driver's window, smiling, her eyes went wide with recognition, and she dropped the tray with a clatter.

Silently Brad swore. Damn if he hadn't forgotten he was a famous country singer.

The girl, a skinny thing wearing too much eye makeup, immediately started to cry. "I'm sorry!" she sobbed, squatting to gather up the mess.

"It's okay," Brad answered quietly, leaning to look down at her, catching a glimpse of her plastic name tag. "It's okay, Mandy. No harm done."

"I'll get you another dog and a shake right away, Mr. O'Ballivan!"

"Mandy?"

She stared up at him pitifully, sniffling. Thanks to the copious tears, most of the goop on her eyes had slid south. "Yes?"

"When you go back inside, could you not mention seeing me?"

"But you're Brad O'Ballivan!"

"Yeah," he answered, suppressing a sigh. "I know."

She rolled a little closer. "You wouldn't happen to have a picture you could autograph for me, would you?"

"Not with me," Brad answered.

"You could sign this napkin, though," Mandy said. "It's only got a little chocolate on the corner."

Brad took the paper napkin and her order pen, and scrawled his name. Handed both items back through the window.

She turned and whizzed back toward the side entrance to the Dixie Dog.

Brad waited, marveling that he hadn't considered inci-
dents like this one before he'd decided to come back home.
In retrospect, it seemed shortsighted, to say the least, but the
truth was, he'd expected to be—Brad O'Ballivan.

Presently Mandy skated back out again, and this time she
managed to hold on to the tray.

"I didn't tell a soul!" she whispered. "But Heather and
Darlene *both* asked me why my mascara was all smeared."
Efficiently she hooked the tray onto the bottom edge of the
window.

Brad extended payment, but Mandy shook her head.

"The boss said it's on the house, since I dumped your first
order on the ground."

He smiled. "Okay, then. Thanks."

Mandy retreated, and Brad was just reaching for the food
when a bright red Blazer whipped into the space beside his.
The driver's door sprang open, crashing into the metal
speaker, and somebody got out in a hurry.

Something quickened inside Brad.

And in the next moment Meg McKettrick was standing
practically on his running board, her blue eyes blazing.

Brad grinned. "I guess you're not over me after all," he said.